**Cathy Williams** can remember reading Mills & Boon books as a teenager, and now that she is writing them she remains an avid fan. For her, there is nothing like creating romantic stories and engaging plots, and each and every book is a new adventure. Cathy lives in London. Her three daughters—Charlotte, Olivia and Emma—have always been, and continue to be, the greatest inspirations in her life.

# CONTRACTED FOR THE SPANIARD'S HEIR

CATHY WILLIAMS

**MILLS & BOON**

First Published in Great Britain 2019
by Mills & Boon, an imprint of HarperCollins*Publishers*
1 London Bridge Street, London, SE1 9GF

 © 2019 Cathy Williams

ISBN: 978-0-263-07940-1

**MIX**
Paper from
responsible sources
**FSC® C007454**

This book is produced from independently certified FSC™ paper
to ensure responsible forest management.
For more information visit www.harpercollins.co.uk/green.

Printed and bound in Great Britain
by CPI Group (UK) Ltd, Croydon, CR0 4YY

# CHAPTER ONE

'SHALL I BRING the girl in now, sir?'

Sprawled back in his swivel chair, Luca Ross looked at his housekeeper, Miss Muller, who was standing to attention by the door.

In short order, he had sacked the nanny, sat his god-son down for a talk to find out what the hell was going on and now, item number three on the agenda, was the girl waiting in the kitchen. It was fair to say that his day had been shot to pieces.

He nodded curtly at his housekeeper, who was as forceful as a sergeant major and one of the few people not intimidated by her aggressive and powerful boss.

'And make sure those hounds don't come with her,' he said flatly. 'Lock them outside if you need to. If it's raining, then they'll get wet. They're dogs. They're built for that. Just make sure they don't destroy any more of my house.'

In the cold confines of his home office—which was better equipped than most commercial offices, with all the accoutrements necessary for him to keep in touch with his myriad companies that spanned numerous time zones—Luca Ross sat back and contemplated this latest, unwelcome development.

He had failed. It was as simple as that. Six months ago, out of the blue, he had inherited a six-year-old cousin once removed, a boy he had briefly met when he had accepted—with cavalier nonchalance, he now realised—the role of godfather.

Luca had few relatives, and certainly none with whom he kept in active contact, and the request, coming from his cousin, had seemed perfectly acceptable. A compliment, even.

His cousin had then set off for foreign shores to seek his fortune, breathtakingly naïve in his assumption that the streets of California were really and truly paved with gold, and Luca had promptly lost touch.

Life was hectic. Emails had been few and far between and his conscience when it came to the role of godfather had been easily soothed by the occasional injection of cash into the bank account he had set up for his godson shortly after his cousin and his young wife had set off to sail the seas and make their fortune.

Job done.

He had not banked on actually being called upon to take charge of anyone, least of all a six-year-old child, but fate, unfortunately, had had other plans.

Jake's parents had been tragically killed in an accident and Luca had been left with a godson who had no place whatsoever in his highly controlled and extremely frenetic life.

Naturally, Luca had done his best and had flung money at the unexpected problem. But now, sitting back in his office while he waited for the tiny, dark-haired thing who had returned his godson two hours earlier, he had to concede that he had failed.

That failure was an insult to his dignity, to his pride

and, more than that, signalled a dereliction of the duty he had blithely taken upon his shoulders when he had accepted the position of godfather.

Once this chaotic mess was brought to a conclusion, he would have to rethink the whole situation or else risk something far worse happening in the not-too-distant future.

What, precisely, the solution to that problem might be, Luca had no idea, but he was confident he would be able to come up with something. He always did.

Standing outside the door, where she had been delivered like an unwanted parcel by the fearsome middle-aged woman with the steel-grey hair and the unsmiling face of a hit man, Ellie wasn't sure whether to knock, push open the door which was ajar or—her favoured option—run away.

She instantly and regrettably ruled out the running away option because right now, in the pouring rain, the dogs she was looking after were mournfully doing heaven only knew what in the back garden of this stupidly fabulous Chelsea mansion. She couldn't abandon them. If she did, she quailed to think what their fate might be. Neither the hard-faced housekeeper nor her cold-as-ice employer struck her as the types who had much time for dogs. They would have no problem tossing all three dogs into the local dogs' home faster than you could say 'local dogs' home'.

She licked her lips. Hovered. Twisted her hands together. Tried hard not to think about the towering, intimidating guy to whom she had spoken briefly an hour and a half previously when she had rung the doorbell to deliver one runaway six-year-old back to his home. She'd had no idea to whom the blond child belonged, but she certainly hadn't envisaged the sort of drop-dead gorgeous man who had greeted them with an expression that could have frozen water. He had looked at her and the dogs and then taken charge of the situation in a manner that had brooked no debate, dispatching her to the kitchen where she had been commanded to *sit and wait; he would be with her shortly.*

She tentatively knocked on the door, took a deep breath and then walked into the room with a lot more bravado than she was currently feeling.

Like the rest of the house she had glimpsed, this room positively screamed *luxury.*

In her peripheral vision, she took in the cool greys, the marble, the built-in bookcase with its rows of forbidding business tomes. On one wall, there was an exquisite little painting that she vaguely recognised. On the opposite wall, there was an ornate series of hand-mounted clocks, all telling different times, and of course the vast granite-and-wood desk on which were three computers, behind which...

'My apologies if you have been kept waiting.' Luca nodded at the leather chair facing his desk, his cool, dark eyes never leaving Ellie's face. When she had shown up at his front door, with Jake in one hand and a series of leads attached to dogs in the other, Luca had thought that he had never seen such a scrappy little thing in his life. Small, slender, with short hair and clothes he associated with the sort of people with whom he had minimal contact. Walkers, ramblers, lovers of great open spaces...

He'd barely been able to see what sort of figure she had because it had been hidden under a capacious jumper that was streaked with muddy paw-prints. Her jeans had been tucked into similarly muddy wellies and she had forgone the nicety of an umbrella as protection against the driving summer downpour in favour of a denim hat from beneath which she had glared at him with unhidden, judgemental criticism.

All in all, not his type.

'Sit. Please.'

'I don't know what I'm doing here, Mr Ross. Why have I been made to hang around, waiting to see you? My whole day has been thrown out of kilter!'

'Tell me about it. And I'm betting that your out-of-kilter day is somewhat less catastrophic than mine, Miss… Edwards, is it? When I left for work this morning, the last thing I anticipated was being called back here because my godson had done a runner.'

'And it was a good job I was there to bring him back!' Ellie stuck her chin out defiantly, recalling in the nick of time that she was really furious with this man, who clearly ran such a rubbish ship on the home front that his godson had absconded, crossing several main roads and endangering his life to get to the park where anything could have happened, because this was London.

Anger felt very good, because the alternative was that unsettling *awareness* in the pit of her stomach because the guy staring at her, as grim-faced as an executioner, was also one of the most ridiculously good-looking men she had ever set eyes on.

An exotic gene pool was evident in the rich bronze of his skin and the midnight darkness of his stunning eyes while his features were perfectly and lovingly chiselled to exquisite perfection. One look at him had been enough to knock the breath out of her body and, sitting here, the effect of those remote, thick-fringed dark eyes on her was threatening to do so again.

'You have no idea how dangerous London can be,' she emphasised, tearing her gaze away from his with visible difficulty. 'A young boy wandering through a park...? That's a disaster waiting to happen.'

'Yes. There is no doubt about that.' Luca sat back and stared at her coldly and thoughtfully. 'Incredibly fortuitous that you were on the scene, ready to return him.'

'Yes. Yes, it was.'

'Should I tell you at this point how fortunate you are that you're not currently being quizzed by the police?'

Ellie stared at him blankly while her brain tried to crank into gear and make sense of what he was saying.

'Police?'

'My initial reaction when my housekeeper phoned to tell me that Jake couldn't be found was to suspect kidnap.'

'Sorry?'

'Look around you, Miss Edwards.' Luca waved his hand carelessly to encompass the luxurious surroundings of his office, where an original Picasso rubbed shoulders with an impressive sculpture of an elongated woman that rested on a glass stand.

Ellie duly looked.

'I have never,' Luca continued, 'considered the necessity for bodyguards—or kidnap insurance, for that matter—but then I have never been in charge of a young and unpredictable child. Had you not shown up when you had, my next phone call would have been to the police, and you would now be sitting here being interrogated by them. However, here you are, and, in answer to your original question, the reason I kept you waiting was because I thought it necessary to establish what role, if any, you played in my nephew's disappearance.'

'I'm sorry, but I'm not following you.'

'In which case, I'll give you a few moments to digest what I've just said. I think, once you've done that, you'll know precisely where I'm going with this.'

'You think that I...that I...'

'I'm not a man who takes chances. I've always found that it pays to take what people tell me with a generous pinch of salt.' Luca shrugged. 'For all I know, you could have lured the boy out with the bait of those three hounds frolicking in my back garden.'

'*Lured him out?* Why on earth would I do that?'

'Now, Miss Edwards, you must surely realise that anyone living in a place like this would be able to pay whatever money you might ask for in return for the safe return of his charge? I won't go so far as to say that you kidnapped the boy. Perhaps it was an opportunity that presented itself, one you decided to take advantage of. Maybe you saw Jake out with the nanny at some point? Noticed where he lived? Temptation and opportunity often have a way of finding one another.'

'That is the *most outrageous* thing I have *ever heard* in my entire life!' Cheeks flaming, Ellie sprang to her feet and then stopped dead when he commanded her to sit back down.

'When you're sitting on a fortune, you find that people will do anything to try and get their hands on some of it. Had the police been called, trust me when I tell you that the line of questioning would have been far more intrusive.'

'Perhaps in your world, Mr Ross, people will do any-thing to try and steal your money—maybe you're surrounded by people who have no scruples—but I can assure you that I'm not interested in getting my hands on any fortune of yours! I had no idea that Jake lived in a place like this. Thank goodness,' she added sarcastically, 'that he was wearing a convenient dog tag so that I knew his address.'

Luca had the grace to flush. 'He's six years old and he's only been in the country for a few months. It was important that he carried some form of identification on him, just in case he ended up lost for some reason. His nanny was instructed never to let him out of her sight, but as you can see for yourself my instructions were lamentably ignored. Jake is a bright boy, but he can't be expected to remember an address he is not familiar with.'

'Do you believe me when I tell you that I just happened to find him in the park, Mr Ross?' Ellie said tightly. 'Because I don't have to stay here and be accused of…being a criminal!'

'Yes.' Luca sighed and twirled the pen on his desk between his fingers before fixing his riveting dark eyes on her. 'I had a word with my godson and it would seem that he got bored. Alicia, the nanny, was on her phone—doubtless on a personal call, which is clearly against the rules—and he thought he'd go and do a little exploring.'

Luca preferred not to dwell on that conversation which, as with most of the conversations with his godson, had been monosyllabic and unsatisfactory.

He had sat on the bed, while Jake had conspicuously refused eye contact, and had done his best to elicit information from him.

'What did you think you were doing, leaving the house without the nanny?' Luca had asked, tempering an inclination to be impatient and critical.

Jake had shrugged.

'Not a good enough answer,' Luca had gritted, which had met with another shrug.

In the end, he had managed to drag a 'I hate it here and I was bored so I went outside to play' from Jake and that had been the sum total of words exchanged.

'It's what six-year-old boys do, unfortunately. They explore, especially when outside looks like more fun than inside.' Her voice was cold. She was still bristling at his insulting insinuation that she might have had something to do with his godson's absconding from the less-than-happy home sweet home. Whatever world Luca Ross inhabited, did he honestly think that everyone around him had some sort of underhand motive and had nothing better to do than to try and access his bank account?

That there wasn't a person out there who wouldn't do what it took to get their hands on what he had?

Except...

She, of all people, was uneasily aware that she should have known what power money and wealth could exert.

She had grown up with the disastrous consequences of a beautiful mother who had been one of those people Luca had talked about; one of those people who would have done anything for money.

Her mother had yearned for that very thing Luca Ross accepted so casually, and that yearning had created a war zone within the Edwards household. Andrea had, as she had made patently clear over the years, married beneath her. She had married a lowly clerk who had failed to rise to the heights she had initially hoped when they had both been young and hopeful. Riven with bitterness and disappointment, she had focused all her energies on ensuring that her youngest daughter, Lily, a beauty like her, could make good on the dreams and aspirations *she* had had to watch wither away.

And the casualty had been Ellie, studious, hardworking and a sparrow to her little sister's shimmering peacock.

Oh, Ellie knew just how damaging the quest for money could be. She had grown up loathing the way people were prepared to behave to get it. Her father had been the one with the strong moral compass and she had adhered to him from a very young age.

The arrogant billionaire sitting in front of her was just the sort of guy she loathed.

The fact that he could sit there and casually accuse her of deliberately trying to con him out of money by snatching his nephew and then returning him in the guise of a Good Samaritan said it all.

'If that's all, Mr Ross…? I have to return the dogs to their owners. I've texted to tell them that there's been a bit of a situation but I can't afford to antagonise any of them.'

'Let me have the addresses of these people. I will ensure that their pets are returned to them.'

'I've already been here for nearly an hour and a half. I have things to do. You said you wanted to talk to me and I'm thinking that you wanted to establish whether you had to bring the police in to arrest me. Now that you've seen I'm not a criminal, I shall leave and take the dogs back to their owners myself. They're tired and they need to be fed.'

'There are a couple of things I still want to straighten out. I can assure you that the dogs will be delivered safely back.'

'By your housekeeper?' Ellie smiled at him without warmth. 'I think she blew the bonding bit when she chucked them out into the pouring rain and locked the door behind them.'

'My orders. I had no intention of letting those dogs drag any more mud into my house than they already had. They're dogs. Enjoying the great outdoors is what they do. My driver has two dogs. He will deliver them, unless you want to hang onto them for another hour or so. Your choice.'

'What else is there to say, Mr Ross? I've told you everything that happened. I saw Jake playing with the dogs and, when I went over, he let slip that there was no adult with him. At first I didn't believe him, because kids are clever when it comes to twisting the truth to get what they want, and I thought that perhaps he wanted to have a bit more time with the dogs, but I very quickly realised that he was telling the truth. He was in that park on his own. Naturally, I was horrified.'

'Naturally.'

'And I got him back here as fast as I could. And, no, I don't want any money for returning your nephew. I'm just relieved that—'

'Yes, got the drift. As for the money element to your statement, why don't we return to that later?'

'There's nothing to return to, Mr Ross.'

'You rescued my godson. I feel we can step away from formalities. Why don't you call me Luca? And you... Ellie, I believe you said?'

Ellie flushed. Luca. Strong, aggressive name for a strong, aggressive male, was the thought that ran through her head. She squashed it flatter than a pancake and gave him a little half-shrug.

'You seem to imply that you're familiar with children.' The dark eyes watching her were careful and speculative as he continued to command the conversation, thinking on his feet as he talked, observing—something he was extremely good at. 'Have you any of your own?'

'I'm twenty-five. I would have to have started very early.'

'And you're not married…'

'How on earth do you know that?'

'No ring on your finger. Jake took to you as well as the dogs. If he hadn't, he would never have allowed you to walk him back to the house. He would have scarpered. It's obvious he trusted you. He was also holding your hand when he returned.' He tilted his head to one side and inspected her in silence for a few long seconds. 'None of this may seem like much of a big deal to you, Ellie, but I can assure you that it is. Since he came over here, he has found it difficult to…settle.'

'Can I ask what happened?'

Luca's initial response to that was to shut down, because answering questions posed by other people was seldom within his remit, unless those questions were work-orientated. Personal questions were off-limits. This was a personal question, but for once he wasn't going to drop the shutters, because he was in a jam and he was beginning to think that part of the solution could be sitting right there in front of him.

'His parents were killed in a car accident,' he intoned flatly. 'Freak situation. They left Jake an orphan. By virtue of the fact that I was Johnny's closest blood relative—his cousin, to be precise, not to mention Jake's godfather—and the fact that Ruby, his wife, had no close family members, I inherited Jake.'

'So you're Jake's second cousin as well as his godfather…'

Luca frowned. 'As I have just said.'

'And yet, despite that connection, things must be a bit strained between you for him to have run away.'

*Was he being called to account?* For a few seconds, Luca's mind went blank because *being called to account* was not something with which he was familiar.

'A bit strained?' he questioned in a voice that would have had grown men quaking, a voice he had perfected over the years, one which was very handy when it came to controlling anyone who had the temerity to breach his barriers.

The slender, dark-haired gamine sitting opposite him wasn't quaking.

'It happens,' she said, her voice rich with sympathy. 'Just because you're family doesn't always mean that the relationship is close.' She thought of her own relationship with her sister, which was anything but close even though, once upon a time, they had been far closer than they were now.

'Jake and his parents,' Luca said heavily, 'went to America to live. Keeping in touch was difficult.'

'I'll bet.'

'I'm an extremely busy man.' Luca heard the irritation in his voice and was exasperated with himself for launching into explanations that were, frankly, unnecessary.

'It wasn't meant as a criticism,' Ellie murmured, lowering her eyes and thinking that that was exactly how it had been meant—because what she was deducing was that Luca would have been way too busy making money to remember some cousin on the other side of the world.

'The fact is that we have both found ourselves in a situation where adjustments have had to be made and Jake has found those adjustments somewhat difficult.'

'Poor, poor kid. No wonder he's had trouble settling down. I've come across that sort of thing a couple of times, usually involving kids who have come to London from another country, and in one instance to stay with a distant relative they really didn't know very well. Adjusting was an issue.'

She sat up straighter, on more solid ground now that she was in possession of a few facts. 'I don't suppose...' she had nothing to lose by speaking her mind '...it's helped that he's been farmed out to a nanny and a housekeeper, and heaven only knows who else, when all he probably needs is one-on-one time with you as the adult responsible for his welfare.'

'Is that a criticism?' Luca asked coldly. 'Because I've been sensing a few of those under the demure replies and the polite questions.'

Ellie dug her heels in and shrugged. 'I can tell you don't appreciate it,' she said eventually, when the silence threatened to become too tense, 'but I'm just speaking my mind. I'm a teacher, and I have quite a bit of experience when it comes to young kids.'

'So you're a teacher? That's very interesting.' Luca dropped his eyes and doodled something on the pad in front of him.

'Is it? Why?'

'I feel I would have worked that out eventually,' he murmured, and she reddened.

'Why is that, Mr Ross?'

'Luca.'

Ellie stared at him, lips tightly pressed together, and just like that Luca smiled.

Her expression—thorough disapproval even though she was let down by having such a delicate, feminine face, all huge green eyes, short, straight nose and a mouth that was a perfect Cupid's bow. The more defiantly she tilted her chin, narrowed her eyes and aimed for severe, the more amused he was.

'I'm not seeing the joke.' Ellie's heart was slamming against her rib cage, and not just because she knew that he was laughing *at* her. That smile was so *sexy* and, just like that, she glimpsed someone other than the ice-cold billionaire who had rubbed her up the wrong way the second she had met him and who represented everything she had no time for.

And this *someone other* was dangerous. She felt it. This *someone other* wasn't just drop-dead gorgeous. He was sinfully sexy, the sort of *sexy* that should come with a health warning.

'You should see your face,' Luca drawled. 'Tight lips, pursed mouth, disapproving eyes. Could you be anything *but* a school teacher?'

He made that sound like a source of amusement instead of consternation, which somehow made his criticism all the more offensive.

'Maybe most of them are too scared,' she snapped with reckless abandon.

'I don't care for that tone of voice.' Cool eyes fastened on her flushed face. He realised that she had signally made no effort to try and impress him from the second she had walked into his house, just as he realised that most people did, which was something he took for granted.

'And I don't care for the fact that you think it's okay to sit there and laugh at me. I'm a teacher, an excellent teacher, and if you think that it's hilarious that I speak my mind then too bad.'

'Not hilarious,' Luca said slowly, speculatively. 'Refreshing.'

His mobile buzzed and he took the call, which lasted a matter of seconds. Not for a second did his eyes leave her face.

Ellie had the strangest sensation of intense discomfort under that scrutiny. It was as if her body was on hyper-alert, sensitive in ways she couldn't quite understand. She felt restless in her own skin and yet frozen to the spot, barely able to breathe.

'The dogs have gone. I'm sure their owners will be overjoyed to have them home.' He sat back and inclined his head to one side. 'Can I ask you something, Ellie?'

Ellie felt that he would anyway, whatever answer she gave, so she tilted her head to one side and didn't say anything.

'Why are you walking dogs when you have a job?'

That wasn't what she had been expecting and she went bright red.

'I don't see what that has to do with anything,' she muttered.

'The nanny has gone.' He changed tack so abruptly that she was left floundering and wrong-footed.

'The nanny…?'

'Second in six months.'

'That can't be a good thing. The poor boy probably needs continuity,' Ellie said when he made no attempt to elaborate on this. 'Children really need defined boundaries and, especially in Jake's situation, stability would be very important.' *Tight lips…pursed mouth…disapproving eyes…* Ellie was impatient with herself for letting him get under her skin, because who cared what the man thought one way or another?

'I fully agree with you. It's been disappointing but what can one do? The first nanny was a middle-aged lady who was clearly out of her depth dealing with Jake. He's extremely clever and very strong-willed underneath that quiet exterior. It would seem that he simply refused to go along with any plan he didn't agree to.' Luca paused. 'He also created such a fuss about going to school that, as it came out in the wash, the woman was browbeaten into keeping him at home on a couple of occasions which, naturally, didn't work.'

'Has he not settled into school life either?'

'It's been a difficult period,' Luca murmured with exquisite understatement.

Confused, because she had no idea where this roundabout conversation was leading, but very much aware that there was a definite destination in sight even though it eluded her at the moment, Ellie stared at Luca with fascination.

Everything about him was compelling, from the graceful, economical movements of his hands when he spoke to the proud angle of his head and the harsh beauty of his features.

For the first time, she was awkwardly conscious of the gaping chasm between them—and not just in the money stakes.

He was so breathtakingly beautiful that he made her aware of her shortcomings, and that was a place she hadn't visited for a long time.

Growing up, she had learned to accept that when it came to looks she was second-best.

Lily was the one with the looks. Like her mother, she was tall, willowy and blonde, her vanilla hair dropping like a waterfall down her narrow back. From the day she'd been born, she had been attracting attention, and that had only become more pronounced as she had grown and eventually matured into a stunningly beautiful adolescent.

With a sister blessed with such spectacular looks, Ellie had quickly learned to fade into the background, developing skills that did not rely on physical appearance. She had studied hard, got A grades in everything, helped out during summers at the local kennels and played as much sport as she could, because being outside the house often beat being inside it.

So it was irritating now to find herself thinking about her looks and wondering what Luca saw when he stared at her with such a veiled expression.

'I had hoped,' Luca said truthfully, 'that Alicia might have worked out. I'd come to the conclusion that it might have been a mistake relying on experience to deal with Jake, without taking into account that experience might come with the downside of being a little too stuffy to handle a kid of six.'

'Mr Ross... Luca... I'm sorry that your nephew hasn't settled over here as well as he might have. I would advise you to try and bond with him a bit more, but I'm sure you'll ignore me. Perhaps, after this little incident, his nanny will be a little more vigilant. Maybe she just needs to get him out and about a bit more. It's the summer holidays and there's an awful lot going on in London at the moment for kids. Or she could even take him out of London. To the seaside, perhaps.'

'That would be difficult,' Luca said gently, when she had finally tapered off into silence, 'considering the nanny has been sacked.'

'Sacked? But why?'

'Why do you think?'

'Yes, well... I'm sure she will have learned from this episode...' Ellie vaguely wondered whether the sacked nanny could take him to some kind of industrial tribunal for unfair dismissal but somehow she couldn't envisage anyone, least of all a young nanny, having the courage to do anything of the sort.

And sadly, whilst the poor girl probably did deserve a second chance, it was fair to say that letting her charge escape did come under the heading of *dereliction of duty*.

'I would hope so but it doesn't matter because it's not my problem.' Luca pushed himself away from the desk and linked his fingers on his washboard stomach. 'My problem isn't what the sacked nanny does now. My problem is what *I* do now...'

# CHAPTER TWO

LUCA HAD REACHED a decision. He'd done what he did best. Faced with a problem, he had brought his natural creativity to the situation, thought on his feet and come up with a solution.

He'd sacked the nanny. He needed cover. And it wasn't going to fall on his shoulders because he didn't have enough hours in the day.

Miss Muller, efficient though she was, could hardly be expected to turn her hand to child minding a six-year-old. She'd never had children and, from the little he had glimpsed of her interaction with Jake, an eagerness to make up for that lack was not there.

And the agency wasn't going to be much help in the immediate future. They were painstaking when it came to the business of sourcing nannies. Leave it with them and he could be collecting his pension before they came up with a replacement, especially given the short, chequered history of the previous two, both sacked.

Cover was staring him in the face. The girl was perfect. He was good when it came to reading people and he could read that this one would be up to the job.

He would lay his cards on the table soon enough but first he would find out as much as he could about her personal circumstances because her personal circumstances could be used to his advantage.

He would at least have to determine her availability.

It didn't occur to him to ask her directly whether she would be able to step into the breach because getting what you wanted always panned out better once you'd got a feel for the lie of the land. A lifetime of dealing with people had given Luca a healthy scepticism when it came to making sure he got the best possible deal from them.

This girl was no gold-digger, but that didn't mean she wouldn't be tempted to try her luck if she thought she could pull a fast one.

'You never told me why you were walking dogs.' He lazily returned to the question he had earlier directed at her. He tilted his big body at an angle that allowed him to watch her closely from under lowered lashes. 'You have a job. I don't know what teachers get paid, but I'm assuming it's not so little that they have to take a begging bowl onto the streets.'

'Walking dogs isn't the same as *taking a begging bowl onto the streets.*'

'Figure of speech. Shouldn't you be enjoying your respite from tetchy kids and classrooms?'

'I...' Ellie reddened. 'I like dogs,' she said lamely. 'And I like walking.'

'And that's very commendable, but you surely must do it because of the money?'

'I... As it happens, I find the additional income very useful.' Ellie heard herself stutter out the truth and immediately told herself that it was nothing to be ashamed about and that she shouldn't let herself be cowed into editing her personality which was, by its nature, open and honest.

'Why?'

'*Why?* Mr Ross, *Luca*, I'm not one of your employees. I don't actually have to tell you anything.'

'Instead of getting worked up because I'm asking you a few questions, you need to sit back and listen to me without interruption for a few minutes.'

Ellie's mouth dropped open.

'You probably want to get back to your house as much as I need to return to work, but there *was* something I wanted to propose to you, and I think you would be open to my suggestion—especially if you tell me that you need money.'

'I never said that I *needed* money.'

'You don't have to but I'm good at joining dots. I heard the anxiety in your voice when you talked to me about reuniting those dogs with their owners. You were apprehensive about upsetting them. You don't want to upset them because, however much you love dogs and love walking, it's not a labour of love for you. Ergo, you need the money.

'Now, don't get me wrong. I don't give a damn what you want the money for—addiction to fine wine, an obsession with designer clothes...or maybe you're saving for a round-the-world cruise. I don't care. It's all the same to me. You have no criminal record, because checks would have been done on you before you became a teacher. Here's the deal.'

He leant forward, palms flattened on the desk. 'I no longer have a nanny and I can't afford to spare the time out for babysitting duties. Miss Muller isn't going to be able to step up to the plate here and I would not ask her to. However, as I said to you, my nephew took to you and that in itself speaks volumes. Combined with the fact that you clearly need the money, we could work together towards a satisfactory solution to my problem.'

Ellie stared at him in a daze. She was accustomed to controlling situations. It was part and parcel of her job, but right now she felt as though she had handed the reins over to someone who was cheerfully steering her in the direction he wanted her to go.

'I'll admit my immediate reaction to you showing up at my front door with my godson was one of instant suspicion.'

Ellie was fascinated by Luca's lack of apology for behaviour that frankly had been pretty outrageous. When she had walked Jake back, she had anticipated gratitude. She had mentally prepared an informative speech about the importance of family and of understanding the psyche of children. It was going to be a severe speech, as befitted the situation. She had even mulled over the possibility that she might step into a quagmire that would necessitate outside intervention. She worked in a school where that sort of thing had occurred on a couple of occasions, although something about Jake had made her think that his family life wasn't going to be a disaster zone. His clothes had been dishevelled and muddy from the dogs but expensive all the same.

She hadn't anticipated a series of events that had seen her told coolly that she could have been hauled down to a police station, accused of staging the whole thing for money and then eventually been given the all-clear without a hint of remorse.

'I got that,' Ellie said tightly as her mind continued to whirr. She couldn't take her eyes off him. He was larger than life in every sense of the word and in his presence every nerve-ending in her body was on red alert, every sense and pulse stretched to breaking point. From the proud angle of his head to the luxuriant dark hair and exotically sculpted features, the man oozed more than just sexuality and it knocked her for six.

And now he was offering her a job?

'Naturally I would do my own background check on you anyway,' he murmured, half to himself.

'You're offering me a job?' Just in case she'd got hold of the wrong end of the stick.

'The circumstances are a little unusual,' Luca admitted. 'It's not in my nature to jump into anything without first testing the water, but I need someone to look after Jake, and sooner rather than later...'

'But you could always just take a couple of weeks off work. Maybe go on holiday with him whilst the agency finds a replacement. If he's had trouble settling down then a holiday might be just the thing he needs.'

'I don't have time for holidays,' Luca said flatly.

'Never?' Ellie asked incredulously, wondering what the point of being rich was if you never took time out to enjoy your hard-earned cash. If *she* had money, then she would travel the world. It was a luxury she had never had.

'There's no time off when you're running a business the size of mine.' Luca shrugged. 'It may sound harsh but I'm simply being realistic.' He leaned back and sighed heavily, with a hint of impatience. 'This escapade has made me realise that Jake needs someone who is not only capable of taking him from A to B and making sure he is fed and watered, but someone with whom he has some kind of bond. He clearly didn't bond with either of the previous nannies, but in the space of a very short time he managed to do that with you, and I'm guessing your experience as a teacher has something to do with that.' He looked at her shrewdly. 'So here we are.'

'I already have a job,' Ellie said. As job offers went, this one certainly hadn't been wrapped up in any pretty packaging. He was in a jam and she was a possible solution. No beating about the bush with any niceties.

'Teaching, and walking dogs for the additional income.'

She decided not to go down the 'needing money' road again. Luca made her nervous and uncomfortable and she couldn't think of anything worse than working for him. 'There's no way,' she said politely, 'that I would ever consider jacking in my full-time job to become a nanny to your godson. I love my job. I enjoy working with lots of different kids.'

He would make a terrible employer. It was obvious that he was as warm and cuddly as a rattlesnake. He thought nothing of getting rid of people who didn't live up to his high expectations and, while he was quick to blame, he didn't seem prepared to accept that he might be the root cause of Jake's behaviour.

Work for him?

She would rather walk on a bed of burning coals. Part of the reason she enjoyed what she did, aside from the satisfaction of working with the kids, was that she really loved the people she worked alongside.

They were on her wavelength. They were all part of the greater caring community who didn't rush to put themselves first.

Luca Ross was part of the cut-throat community who thought nothing of taking what they wanted whatever the cost. He was arrogant, ruthless and manipulative. She'd been in his company for a handful of hours and already she felt wrung out.

'I'm not talking about a long-term position,' he clarified, still fully confident that he was going to get what he wanted because, frankly, he always did. 'Of course, a suitable nanny will be found in due course, but that's going to take time, and this time around I will have more input to the procedure than previously.'

Ellie was making a mental list in her head of all the things she disliked about him and she tacked this new one on. *He probably left choosing the nannies to his secretary because he was too busy and couldn't be bothered...*

'I'm sorry,' she said, standing up so that he could take the hint that their conversation was at an end. Her body broke out in light perspiration as he slowly rose to his feet. He strolled towards her, in no hurry.

His long, lean body oozed latent strength and suffocating masculinity. She could almost see the flex of sinew and muscle under the charcoal-grey trousers and the white shirt, which he had cuffed to the elbow. His forearms were liberally sprinkled with dark hair. She wondered whether his chest would likewise be sprinkled with dark hair and she furiously stopped herself in crazy mid-thought.

He cast an ominous shadow as he finally paused to stand in front of her, and Ellie had to will herself not to cower.

The mental checklist of things she disliked about the man was growing by the second. Not only did he think he could get whatever he wanted but he was not averse to using sheer brawn and intimidation tactics to get there.

'Sorry?'

'I'm not interested in working for you.' She cleared

her throat and their eyes collided, causing the air to rush out of her body in a whoosh. 'I appreciate the offer, but you're better off going back to the agency, and maybe taking more of a hands-on approach this time, because you seemed to imply that you hadn't on the previous occasions.'

'How can you appreciate my offer when you haven't heard the details?'

'I don't need to.'

'Care to tell me why?'

'I know you think that you can get whatever you want because you're rich, but you can't.' She tore her eyes away with difficulty. He was standing so close to her that she could breathe in whatever woody, intensely masculine aftershave he was wearing.

Breathing was proving to be a problem. It was unnerving. She forced herself to remain calm and composed because he was just standing there; he wasn't trying to prevent her from leaving the room. She remembered how to breathe and then looked at him.

'Jake ran away for a reason.' Her voice, thankfully, did not betray the utter turmoil his proximity was bringing on. 'Okay, so maybe he didn't like the nanny very much, or perhaps he got bored and decided to venture out, but the bottom line is that there's obviously something missing on the home front and that something can only be provided by you.'

'We're going round in circles.'

'Because we're on completely different wavelengths.' She cleared her throat and wished that he would back off by even a couple of inches so that she could get her act together. 'And that's just one reason why I could never work for you. We're from different worlds.'

'Since when do people have to think alike in order to have a satisfactory working arrangement?'

'It matters to me,' Ellie persisted. Since she had nothing to lose, she said, bluntly, 'I don't like what you stand for. I'm not into money and I don't approve of people who focus all their energy on making it. I'm happy doing what I'm doing, and I wish you all the best in your search for a replacement for the nanny you sacked.'

Luca stared at her in silence then he nodded slowly.

He backed away, leaving a cool void behind him. Desperate to leave only seconds earlier, Ellie now hovered uneasily. He had moved back to the desk but was now perched on the edge and was watching her with a thoughtful expression.

'So...' She licked her lips nervously.

'You were on your way out?'

'Yes, I was!' She pulled open the door and an odd thought suddenly sprang into her addled brain—*this will be the last time you set eyes on this man.* She blinked, surprised and bemused at the discomfiture that thought provoked out of nowhere.

Ellie thought he might have tried to stop her, one last stab at persuading her to hear him out, and she was disconcerted to find that she was almost disappointed when he remained in the office while she let herself out of the house, pausing and looking up the stairs on her way out.

Should she try and find Jake? Say goodbye? She wanted to. In a short space of time, he had touched her with his shy overtures of friendship.

No. She'd already become way too involved in his backstory. She'd done her good deed for the week and delivered him back to his home and it was doubtful she would lay eyes on him again.

Whatever nanny Luca got, Ellie's money was on the poor girl being monitored more closely than a convict on parole. She would be manacled to the poor child while Luca carried on making money and kidding himself that he was being a good guardian by flinging cash at the problem that had landed on his doorstep.

Hateful and obnoxious, she thought, barely aware of the walk back to the park and then on to the nearest bus because she was so busy thinking of him.

Ellie shared a house with three other girls. Every time she approached the front door, she recalled the far nicer little place she had rented previously where she had been able to relax in peace; where she hadn't had to jostle for space in the fridge; any time she wanted to herself now had to be spent in a bedroom that was only just about big enough for a bed, a chest of drawers and a wardrobe that was a whisker away from being held together by masking tape. But needs must.

She wondered, but only briefly, whether she should have listened to whatever offer Luca had been prepared to put on the table...

Twenty-four hours later, Ellie was on her way back home when she noticed a long, sleek, black car pull away from the kerb, picking up speed and then slowing down until it was right alongside her.

The persistent rain of the past couple of weeks had stopped and, at a little after six-thirty in the evening, a watery sun was trying to remind everyone that it was still summer.

The road was quiet, practically deserted, and with a flare of panic she quickened her steps, only almost to collide into the passenger door of the car which had been flung open, barring her path.

'Hop in, Ellie.'

She recognised the voice instantly and, when she peered inside, her heart did a quick flip and her breathing hitched. Luca was the last person she had been expecting to see again.

The tinted windows had prevented her from seeing the driver and now she wondered how on earth he had managed to do that? Show up just when she was on her way back to her house. Did he have some sort of telepathic X-ray vision?

She blinked, her mouth opening and shutting while Luca looked at her in total silence.

'How did you find me?'

'Hop in.'

'No!'

'Don't slam the door. Just get in the car and listen to what I have to say.'

'How did you find me?' she repeated, reluctant to get in the car yet not wanting to draw attention to herself. She slid into the passenger seat and slammed the door behind her.

In the enclosed space, she was uneasily conscious of the raw sexuality that had accosted her the last time she had been in his company. He was so staggeringly *male*, so devoid of any soft side, so unapologetically masculine.

She looked at him and didn't know whether it was because he had been on her mind, or whether it was just the shock of seeing him when she hadn't expected to, but her body was suddenly filled with a disturbing electric charge.

Her nipples pinched, scraping against her tee shirt because she seldom wore a bra except to work. What was the point when there was precious little to hold in place? And there was a stickiness between her legs that horrified her, made her want to slam her thighs together tightly.

'Don't forget, I know where your dog-walking clients live,' Luca intoned smoothly. 'I asked them whether you were out with their dogs. Actually, I struck jackpot with owner number one. You're a creature of habit, Ellie. Same routine. It was a pretty simple process of deduction that you would be heading back to your house around now. Mrs Wilson was kind enough to let me have your address. She also gave me your mobile number but I thought it best if I surprised you.'

'She had *no right* to hand over my private details!'

'Maybe she could tell at a glance that I wasn't a homicidal maniac.'

'That's not the point.'

'Which is your house?'

'I don't want you in my house!'

'Then we can sit here and have this conversation,' he said calmly. He killed the engine and reclined in the chair, angling his big body so that he was facing her.

'We've covered everything there is to say. I'm not going to work for you.'

'You've moved.'

'I beg your pardon?'

'You never used to live in this part of London. You used to rent a tidy little flat in West London, but you gave that up two months ago so that you could move to this area which is, at the very best, dodgy.'

'How did you find all of that out?'

'I can find out anything I want to,' Luca told her without batting an eyelid. 'And I wanted to find out about you because I want you. You're saving money, and a brief background check leads me to believe that it's because you're helping your father out of a hole.'

Ellie stiffened, shocked and dismayed. How far was his reach?

'Tell me about it,' he said, but his voice was curiously gentle. 'And don't let your feelings for me and your pride get in the way of your common sense, Ellie. Like I told you, we can help one another. As business arrangements go, this could be an extremely rewarding one for both of us. I need someone there for Jake. Did you know that he's asked after you?'

Suspicion poured out of every pore in Ellie's body but that question, tacked on at the end, made her hesitate, even though she suspected that he was a man who would work the cards in his hand any way he chose if it could get him what he wanted.

You didn't get to the top by being kind and caring and making allowances for the weak and feeble. You got to the top by being ruthless, and he was at the very top.

'It's the first conversation I think I've had with Jake since he came over here. Or, at least, the first conversation that wasn't like squeezing blood from a stone.'

Ellie opened her mouth to inform him that she wasn't interested, and besides she resented the fact that he had been investigating her behind her back, but instead she heard herself say, 'What do you mean?'

'We've barely spoken. I've had reports from the nannies but the times we've sat down together over a meal, he's only managed to mutter a few monosyllabic answers to the questions I've asked. This morning, he asked after you, and after those mutts you introduced him to. He wanted to know whether he would be able to return to the park so that he could walk with you.'

His expression was shuttered but Ellie was good at reading body language and what she was seeing was genuine emotion from a man who probably found it difficult to express himself in terms of feelings and who was at a loss with a situation he couldn't control.

'This would not be a permanent position,' he told her softly, shifting, because a car was not the most comfortable of places in which to have a protracted conversation. 'It would be a matter of a few weeks, no more than the duration of the summer holidays, during which time you could perhaps help source a replacement nanny for Jake. I think your input would be helpful on that front. It's clear you have an instinctive empathy with children, which is something I clearly lack.'

Ellie opened her mouth and he raised his hand.

'No, allow me to finish before you start digging your heels in.' He shot her a crooked smile and Ellie blinked because, shorn temporarily of that authoritarian streak in him that she had previously glimpsed, he was curiously *human*. It was unnerving.

'I could have found out the details of whatever commitment you may have towards your father, but I stopped short of that because it doesn't matter, and I also felt that if you wanted to fill me in then you would. I will pay you enough to more than cover the entire debt your father has incurred.'

'That's a crazy assurance,' Ellie said shakily. Her eyes dropped to where he was resting his hand lightly on the gear shaft and she inconsequentially thought what shapely hands he had.

'My pockets are shockingly deep,' Luca returned without a trace of false modesty. He paused and inclined his head to one side. 'What happened? Do you want to talk about it?'

The vision of being released from the stranglehold of a debt that would take her years to clear dangled in front of Ellie's eyes like an oasis in the desert.

'If you'd rather not go into the details, then that's fine. All I want to know is this: are you prepared to consider my offer? In return for a handful of weeks working for me, your father will never have to worry about his debts again. You don't have to like me to agree to this. That doesn't enter the equation. All you have to do is ask yourself whether you're willing to prolong your father's unhappy situation because of misplaced pride.'

As trump cards went, Ellie knew that he had pulled out the ace of spades. Her father was stressed beyond belief and frankly so was she.

Did she want him to know the situation? Ellie already knew that she would agree to what he wanted. He'd somehow managed to find the precise spot where his appeal would hit pay dirt.

'It would be a relief to clear my father's debts,' Ellie said stiffly.

'Before you continue, do you want to carry on this conversation in your house? I'm too big to sit in this car indefinitely. I need to stretch my legs.'

'I share the place with other girls.' She involuntarily grimaced. 'But I guess we could go to a pub. There's one not far from here. I could direct you.'

Having secured the deal, Luca had no intention of letting the grass grow under his feet. They were in the pub with a bottle of chilled wine in front of them within fifteen minutes.

'So…?' he pressed urgently.

'My dad has found himself in a bit of a pickle.' She opened up, because she did want him to know more than just the bones of why she was taking this job. He'd found out so much about her that he could easily have found out the entire story and the fact that he hadn't softened her impression of him. Just a little. If she chose not to explain anything, she knew that he wouldn't try to find out off his own bat but, for some reason, she didn't want him to be left with the suspicion that her father had blown away his savings on rubbish.

'He got taken in by a scam on the Internet. He didn't admit to what had happened for a while. In fact, I only found out because I happened to come across a letter from the bank he had left on the console table in the sitting room. When I asked him what was happening, he admitted to everything. The bills have been piling up and he hasn't been able to meet his mortgage payments for the past few months. He's been having panic attacks.'

She looked down quickly. 'Apologies,' she said huskily. 'My dad and I are very close and I can't bear to think what he must have been going through. Anyway, of course I earn enough to keep body and soul together, but I've had to move into somewhere smaller temporarily. It's been very stressful and you should know that if it weren't for…this situation there is no way I would be sitting here having this conversation.' She looked at Luca, her green eyes challenging.

The clarity of her gaze was so disconcerting that for a few seconds words failed him.

He was staring at someone from another planet. He had offered her an easy, hassle-free job and instead of biting his hand off and naming her price she had turned him down. She was only accepting the offer now because she would have been insane to refuse it.

Luca was accustomed to women who accepted his generosity without batting an eyelid. He was made of money and he had never yet come up against any woman who didn't enjoy spending some of it when it was on offer.

He hadn't cared why she'd needed money when he had first suggested the job. He'd been confident that she would snap at the chance to get her hands on some to fund whatever lifestyle had left her in debt. He'd assumed a credit card crisis and had banked on her trying to manoeuvre to get the maximum out of him.

He was quietly pleased that he hadn't been able to buy her.

'Tell me how much your father owes,' he said, not beating around the bush, and Ellie reddened and hesitated.

'Do you think I'm going to laugh because he's been the victim of a scam?'

She didn't answer that, instead naming a figure that seemed so huge to her that she looked away in embarrassment.

'Naturally I don't expect you to cover that stupid amount...'

Luca told her what he was willing to pay her, and for once in his life he wasn't interested in driving a hard bargain.

The woman had such fundamental integrity that he was surprised to discover a side to him that wasn't utterly cynical. Born into wealth, Luca had seen from the sidelines how ugly the pursuit of money could be after his mother had died. As an eligible middle-aged widower, his father had become a magnet for women from the ages of twenty to seventy. Many of the women, having admitted defeat with his father, had turned their attentions to him, even though Luca had been a mere boy of seventeen at the time.

His own experiences as an adult had hardly served to change his opinion that there wasn't a woman alive who wouldn't do whatever it took when the stakes were high.

Luca didn't mind. He was happy to be lavish with the women he dated but he had no intention of settling down with any of them. He had no intention of settling down, full-stop.

He was fascinated by Ellie's clear-eyed gaze as their eyes met.

Predictably, she was staggered by the sum he was willing to pay. Even more predictably, she hotly refused to allow him to part with such a vast amount of cash.

'You're overreacting,' he dismissed, reaching to top her glass up. 'I'm not offering you the crown jewels...'

'As good as. It goes against my nature to accept a sum as large as that.'

'And it goes against my nature to be stingy when it comes to a situation like this. You'll be doing me a service, and I'm a man who rewards good service.'

A quiver of excitement rippled through her as their eyes met and tangled. This was a business arrangement, but right now it felt like an adventure...

# CHAPTER THREE

THE FOLLOWING DAY, Ellie finally made contact with her sister.

Lily had called their father the night before and it hadn't taken him long before he phoned Ellie to tell her all about their conversation. But by then Ellie was on her way out to meet Luca for dinner. He would have her contract of employment and had told her that it was essential she knew what was expected of her. Ellie thought that top of the agenda would be not making personal calls while her charge slipped out of the house.

'Did she leave a number, by any chance?' Ellie asked when there was a break in the conversation.

She was going to be late for dinner but if she didn't talk to Lily now then there was no guarantee that she would talk to her at all. Over the years as Lily had pursued fame and fortune, using her incredible looks to open doors, she and Ellie had grown increasingly distant. It took a lot of will power to resist the temptation to let things slide until their contact was reduced to birthday cards and polite conversation over the turkey with their father on Christmas day.

Ellie had no time to beat about the bush.

'Did Dad mention anything…er…about his situation

over here?' she asked bluntly, because the long-distance call was costing her money, and if she didn't stop her sister in mid flow then she would have to spend the entire phone call listening to Lily wax lyrical about all the exciting things happening in her life and the agents who were hunting her down with scripts for movies.

'What situation?' her sister questioned cautiously, so Ellie explained.

She decided that throwing out hints wasn't going to work. 'I thought that since you've found your feet over there you might think about helping me out, Lily. I earn a teacher's salary and I don't have to tell you that it's not much...'

'*You* chose to be a teacher,' Lily snapped defensively. 'So please don't tell me to start feeling sorry for you because you haven't got any money!'

'This isn't about me, Lily. It's about Dad. I've had to take...er...another job to help raise money to clear his debts, but if you could contribute then it would give me some flexibility...when it comes to accepting the offer. Luca will clear the debt but obviously it goes against my pride to accept that level of generosity.'

'What job?' Lily asked curiously. 'Luca? Who's Luca?'

In a mad rush to leave, Ellie briefly explained the situation, that Luca was a Spanish businessman who had hired her to look after his godson for the summer. Lily knew where she stood when it came to money. She would know that accepting such a vast sum of cash would have been tough.

'Oh, for God's sake,' Lily said, although her voice was more thoughtful now. 'Stop with the pride thing and just accept what's on the table. Jeez, the guy is obviously loaded and he needs you to look after the kid. Instead of beating yourself up about it, you should be trying to suss whether you can't get more out of him! Anyway, I can't commit to anything, Ellie, and even if I could I'd be nuts to hand over hard-earned cash when there's some rich guy willing to clear all Dad's debts for a few weeks of playing happy families with his kid.'

So that was that.

Despite the fact that her sister was in the enviable position of having producers banging on her door, she was being true to who she was and refusing to help.

In a rush, Ellie barely glanced at herself in the mirror before flying out of the house.

She was meeting Luca at an Italian bistro in Covent Garden. He had only ever seen her in clothes used to walk dogs, but this was going to be a more formal meeting, and she had dressed accordingly, in the same outfit she pulled out of the wardrobe for parents' meetings. A neat grey skirt, a white blouse and a pair of ballet pumps.

It was an outfit that reminded her of the businesslike nature of their relationship, and for that Ellie was grateful, because when she thought of him her mind started playing games, and what she saw in her head wasn't someone in a suit discussing terms and conditions and holding a fountain pen, it was a man with smouldering sexiness and a smile that could give her goose bumps.

She was half an hour late by the time she stepped into the bistro and looked round her, spotting Luca instantly.

She smoothed down her skirt and took a few seconds to gather herself. The restaurant was busy, with every table filled, and despite the casual sense of waiters hurrying with trays, the open-plan kitchen and the unfussy furnishings, Ellie could tell that the food would cost a fortune.

The clientele was all well-heeled. The food passing her on plates was delicate, artistic creations.

She weaved her way towards Luca and, the closer she got, the more nervous and self-conscious she felt. Her outfit, which had seemed sensible and appropriate when she had put it on an hour earlier, felt cheap and drab and she slid into her chair with a palpable feeling of relief.

'You're late,' Luca opened.

Ellie's initial reaction was to snipe back at him. Her glass-green eyes were narrowed as he glanced at his watch and then relaxed back in the chair to look at her.

Unlike the other people in the restaurant, who were all clearly kitted out in designer gear, Luca looked as though he had dressed in a hurry and without any thought for the end result. His dark hair was combed back and there was a scraping of stubble on his chin. Yet it suited him—he looked even more dangerous with a five o'clock shadow and her nervous system went into free fall.

He was in black. Black tee shirt. Black jeans. Loafers without socks.

Her mouth was suddenly parched and she gulped down some of the water that had been poured into a glass in front of her. A glimpse of her prissy grey skirt was a timely reminder of why she was sitting in this up-market bistro.

And she also realised that his observation was pertinent. If she was going to be working for him, then punctuality was going to be important.

'I'm sorry,' she said, composing herself. 'I was delayed by a phone call. My sister phoned and I haven't spoken to her in quite a while. I couldn't brush her off.'

'Your sister? For some reason I thought that you were an only child.'

'Lily lives in America.'

Luca picked up something in her voice and he inclined his head and waited. This woman was going to be a key part of his life for the next few weeks. Two or three at the very least but almost certainly longer. The contract sitting in the envelope in his pocket offered a clever inducement should she need to stay longer than she might have anticipated. A sliding scale of pay, rising with each week over a two-week tide mark. Irresistible to someone who needed the cash.

Under normal circumstances, he wouldn't be sitting here right now. When it came to employees, it was pretty simple. He paid them well and they either did their job well, and were further rewarded, or else they didn't and they were booted out.

But the last nanny had been a learning curve for Luca. Normal rules didn't apply when it came to something as personal as his godson.

He had hired Alicia, paid her handsomely but he had taken his eye off the ball. In other words, he had treated her the same as he would have treated any of the people who worked for him.

And where had it got him? A runaway child who had had the good luck to be found and delivered back safely by a woman who was obviously charity and goodwill on two legs.

This time round, he was going to have to liaise with the woman looking after Jake and not simply rely on reports, emails and a debrief once a fortnight.

If he was going to have a more hands-on approach, then it would pay actually to find out about her. He needed her to feel comfortable with him because, if she did, she would be a lot more relaxed and forthcoming.

As things stood, she felt about as comfortable with him as a minnow felt in the company of a shark. He knew that. She didn't like him, she disapproved of him, and she'd only taken the job because he had done what he knew how to do so well. He'd put her in a position of being unable to refuse what was on the table.

Luca knew the power of money and he knew how to use it to his advantage.

But you couldn't buy trust and you couldn't buy openness and he would need both if he was to make headway with Jake—and that was what he needed to do.

'Whereabouts?'

'Los Angeles, as a matter of fact. Or at least,' Ellie couldn't help tacking on in the name of perfect honesty, 'I'm assuming that's where she is.'

'Do I hear the sound of the pot calling the kettle black?' Luca asked coolly. 'If I recall, you were pretty vocal on the subject of my losing touch with my cousin when he moved with his family to the very same place your sister now lives. Coincidentally they both ended up in America...'

'Not really. Lots of people go there because they see it as a land of opportunity.'

'But you weren't tempted?'

'I... I don't chase dreams. I'm too grounded.' Ellie flushed. 'Lily and I are very different. Anyway, to get back to what you said, my sister was the one who lost touch with me,' she said uncomfortably. 'Not the other way around.' For some reason, she didn't want to carry on talking about Lily. She remembered the curiosity in her sister's voice when she had mentioned Luca and the huge amount of money he was paying her, enough to clear their father's debt. 'This is a brilliant place.' She looked around her but she could feel his dark, penetrating gaze boring into her. 'You can imagine that, on a teacher's salary, this kind of restaurant is way out of my league.'

A waiter came and Luca gave his order without bothering with the menu, which he hadn't opened, while Ellie made a deal of scrutinising hers and picking what she wanted carefully.

'I have a stake in this place,' he said, casting his eye around him briefly. 'A decade ago, I decided to dabble in the restaurant business, so I bought a few failing ones to add to my portfolio. This was one of them.'

'Right,' Ellie mumbled. 'Of course. It's really important to have a varied portfolio, I've found.'

Luca burst out laughing, then he sipped his wine and was still smiling as he looked at her. 'Is that why you chose to teach? Because your sister was the one who had the monopoly on dream-chasing?'

Startled because he was closer to the truth than he probably imagined, Ellie stared at him for a few seconds. 'Like I said, I'm grounded. I don't have that risk gene in me that's willing to take a chance that everything's going to work out the way I want it to.' Ellie wondered why that made her sound so dull. She was no different from the majority of the human race.

She looked at him with a trace of defiance but his expression was bland and, when he next spoke, it was to change the subject. He had the contract, he told her, fishing it out of his pocket and sliding the envelope towards her.

'We said two to four weeks. I think it's possible that it might be longer. The longer it is, the more you'll be paid.'

Ellie opened the envelope and read the contract. It couldn't have been more straightforward but the sums of money involved made her feel even more uncomfortable now because it was all officially written down, waiting for her signature.

'The job isn't worth what you're willing to pay me,' she said simply and Luca clicked his tongue impatiently.

'We've been over this.'

'I know, but seeing the amount now, in black and white…'

'You need to dump the social conscience, Ellie, or else we'll be having this conversation on a loop, and it's not going to get either of us anywhere. Take the money and run. That's what any sensible person would advise.'

'You'd probably have a lot in common with my sister. You both think along the same lines because that was exactly what she said.' Plus, she thought absently, looking at the lean, beautiful lines of his face, he would probably do what every other guy did when they were confronted with Lily—he would want her.

Ellie thought that she had grown out of feelings she had had when she'd been an impressionable adolescent but now, suddenly, as though Pandora's box had been opened, they all flew out at her and she blinked in dismay.

Lily had always stolen the limelight, but that had been fine. It had only been less fine when she had stolen the one and only guy Ellie had been serious about.

Serious, hard-working, head-firmly-screwed-on Paul had been such a sensible choice and Ellie had liked him a lot. He had been the PE instructor in one of the local schools and she had met him on a night out with some friends. They'd got along and then, of course—oh, why hadn't she seen it coming?—he had been introduced to Lily and Lily had done what she had always done. She had charmed him. She had paraded in front of him in next to nothing, long, slim legs everywhere, blonde hair tousled, blue eyes wide and innocent.

'He actually asked me out,' Lily had said later. 'So really, I did you a favour, because if you'd ended up with him then it wouldn't have lasted. Besides, he was boring.'

The fact that Ellie had not suffered serious heartache following the break-up didn't detract from her annoyance that her sister had had no qualms about proving the point that she was prettier, sexier and more appealing to the opposite sex. After that, Ellie had quietly determined that she would keep any involvement with guys under wraps until she was sure that they were interested in *her* for who she was.

That hadn't been difficult because none had appeared on the horizon since. She had backed away from involvement with the opposite sex because it was easier than risking disappointment.

She was annoyed at the direction of her thoughts and even more annoyed when Luca asked casually, 'If your sister is on the other side of the world making her fortune, why have you been walking dogs to help pay off your father's debts?'

'Because…'

'Got it. So, moving on, you'll have to sign the contract. That will include an agreement to extend cover as necessary.'

'I haven't signed up to an indefinite situation…' *What had he meant by 'got it'?*

'I'm not asking for anything beyond the official school summer holidays—and have a look at the fine print. Stay on and you'll retire with enough money to do more than pay off your father's debts.'

He handed her a pen and nodded. 'You're doing me a favour, Ellie,' he said quietly. 'I'm not just paying you to look after Jake because I've sacked the last nanny and I'm in a tight corner. I'm paying you to be much more than a competent babysitter. I'm paying you because I think you'll be able to bond with Jake and I know that he's going to benefit from that.'

Ellie saw the raw sincerity in Luca's face and any hesitation was wiped out of her mind faster than dew melting on a summer morning. She signed the paper and shoved it back to him.

'Did you mean all that?' she asked, 'Or were you just making sure that you got what you wanted?'

'You think I'm ruthless enough to lie in order to get what I want?'

'Probably,' she said truthfully, and he delivered another of those rare, utterly charming half-smiles that made her thoughts go into a tailspin.

'Lying's not my style,' Luca told her. 'I don't need to use underhand tactics to get what I want in life. I've always found that the art of persuasion is far more successful.'

'And an ability to throw money at a problem.'

Luca shrugged. 'Money talks and usually has the loudest voice. Now, when will you be able to start?'

Since she had nothing planned for the long summer holidays—having assumed that they would be filled with the joys of dog walking to earn some money and perhaps, if push came to shove, some bar work, which she thought she would have rather enjoyed—the answer was *immediately*, but she took her time giving it a lot of undue thought.

'I should go and visit my father before I start,' she answered. 'I'm going to have to explain how it is that I'm suddenly in a position to pay off all his debts, and that's a conversation best had face to face.'

'Understood. Want me to accompany you to do the explaining?'

'No!' Horror laced her voice and she looked at him in alarm.

'Why not?' Luca asked bluntly, irritated by her reaction, because since when had women rejected the offer of his company?

'My father would be astounded if you showed up and he was told that you and I had worked out a deal whereby you were going to be paying me a fortune for looking after your godson for a few weeks.'

'Why?'

'Because…you're not the sort he would ever associate me coming into contact with, far less doing business with.'

'Ah. I'm not the sort you would get along with…unlike the elusive sister. We're back to the sliding scale of your disapproval, are we?'

'It's just easier if I handle this on my own. But thanks for the offer.'

'How long do you intend to stay there?'

'A couple of days at most and then I can start.'

'I should tell you that my preference would be for you to live in, Ellie. I can't always account for my working schedule and it's going to be a nuisance having to find someone who can fill in when necessary. Naturally, you will be compensated.'

'I'm not sure about that,' Ellie muttered, flushing. She thought of the discomfort of her shared house and, when their eyes met, she had a sneaking suspicion that he could read her mind.

He said, 'You'll have your own suite on the top floor. I assure you it will be very comfortable. Very quiet.'

Ellie had missed quiet. She'd never realised how important that was until she'd been thrown into the situation of sharing her space.

'Okay,' she agreed. 'On one condition.'

Luca raised his eyebrows in a question and she told him firmly, 'No extra money. Please. You're already paying me enough to do something that I will enjoy doing anyway.'

*The spendthrift and the saver*, Luca thought with curiosity. *One seeking fame and fortune in America, the other teaching and working her butt off to clear debts her father had incurred.* In his head, a picture was being put together, and for the first time he was genuinely interested in knowing the dynamics behind the relationship between the woman sitting opposite him and her family.

He felt the stirrings of something inside him. Something novel. His love life had become all too predictable and, yes, whilst he enjoyed the predictability, and certainly wouldn't have traded it for anything out of his control, with predictability came a certain amount of boredom.

He'd been celibate for the past two months and the last woman he had dated had only been on the scene for a few weeks. He couldn't really remember what she looked like although he knew that she had run to type—beautiful, blonde, leggy and very amenable. He hadn't been interested in her backstory, although she had insisted on filling him in anyway.

And since then? His libido had gone on holiday.

Luca sat back and looked at Ellie, his lush lashes veiling his expression.

God only knew where she had bought her outfit. Had she specifically looked for something designed to do absolutely nothing for the female form?

And yet the delicacy of her features was strangely arresting, and the fact that he wanted to find out more about her wasn't just about him knowing that he needed to get her onside if the situation with Jake were to work out. She sparked his interest. Her unwillingness to confide spurred on his curiosity. Her lack of interest in his money tickled him pink. She wasn't impressed and she didn't bother to pretend, and that seemed to fire up his jaded soul.

'Now that you're working for me,' he drawled, 'you'll find certain things will be at your disposal. I'll arrange a driver to take you to see your father.'

'My father doesn't live in London.'

'I don't care if he lives in Glasgow. You will also have the services of my driver on tap for when you need to go out with Jake. In addition, I will deposit a sizeable amount of money into your account which you can use when it comes to paying for anything Jake might want or need.'

'Anything?'

'Anything.' Luca shrugged nonchalantly. 'Money is no object.'

Ellie drew in a deep breath and tried hard not to be intimidated by the powerhouse sitting across from her. Everything inside her reacted to him in ways that were embarrassing and unwanted. He wasn't the type of man she could ever be remotely interested in, yet her body went up in flames when she was around him, and that unnerved her. How could she be so uncontrolled in her responses? She'd never been that way and, especially after the debacle with her last boyfriend, she had firmly put the lid on her emotions—not that Paul had roused anything like the idiotic sensations Luca seemed to. That had been a measured relationship, which she had liked. If she had been cautious then, well, she was even more cautious now, so why did sitting within touching distance of Luca make her feel all hot and bothered?

The bottom line was that she was going to have to get her act together because this was a business arrangement and there was no room within any business arrangement for a disobedient body. Luca was a staggeringly good-looking man and the fact that she was so keenly aware of him on a physical level just said something about her hormones. They were in full working order. She should be thankful for that, considering they had done a disappearing act after Paul had left the scene. It was good to know that she was *normal*, and maybe when she was back at work she would think about jumping back into the dating scene. This time round she would make sure that whoever she dated wasn't into leggy blondes.

'Now that you've told me all the terms and conditions about my employment,' she said carefully, 'there are just a few things *I* would like to say.'

Luca's eyebrows flew up and she took a deep breath because she knew that, given half a chance, he would tread all over her and the whole point of this exercise would be lost. It didn't matter how much *she* bonded with Jake, it was far more important that *he* did, and throwing money around like confetti wasn't the way to do it.

'Have you sat down with Jake and actually talked to him about what happened?'

'The runaway episode?'

'The loss of his parents. That episode.'

Luca flushed darkly. 'I thought it best not to bring that up because it's sure to revive bad memories. It's better to move on from that place.'

Ellie held his stare. Food had come somewhere along the line but she had been so preoccupied with the conversation that she had hardly been aware of eating what was on her plate. Now, plates cleared, Luca dismissed a hovering waiter who wanted to find out about dessert.

'I disagree,' Ellie told him firmly, ignoring the way his mouth tightened in automatic rejection of the criticism. 'Just because you don't talk about it doesn't mean that it's all going to disappear. It was something momentous. He's only young, but you can mention his parents naturally so that the subject doesn't become taboo. Have you any pictures of them?'

'I...' Did he have any pictures? All their worldly goods had been shipped back to him and he had had the lot put into the attic. He hadn't checked to see what was there and had thought that at some point in the future, when he had time, he would go through it all. That thought had come and gone and he had done nothing about it.

Ellie was looking at him curiously.

'You don't know?'

'It's not that shocking.' For once on the back foot, Luca shifted irritably, his fabulous eyes pinned to her face. 'I haven't had time to go through the crates that were shipped over,' he muttered.

'You're busy.'

'Is that a criticism?'

'It's an observation.' Ellie paused. 'And if we're going to have a successful working relationship then I have to feel that I can be honest and truthful with you when it comes to Jake.'

Luca lifted both hands in a typically Spanish gesture that could have indicated impatience, annoyance, resignation or a combination of all three. Accompanied as this gesture was by a scowl, Ellie thought that it probably wasn't resignation, but that was tough.

'Feel free,' he delivered smoothly. 'I'm all ears.'

'The first thing you should have done should have been to go through those possessions one by one. There are probably all sorts of things there that would have been cherished by Jake, that would have made him feel more secure in an alien environment. He's still very young. He would have had toys that have been with him probably since he was born.'

Luca looked at her in stony silence but she ignored it. So what if he thought she was a prissy schoolmarm who disapproved of pretty much everything about him?

'Also, what about photos?'

'Do photos exist any more?'

'Then his parents' computers or mobile phones, or any place where digital photos might have been stored.'

'I...' Luca was about to repeat what he had said, that time was a valued commodity and he just hadn't got round to finding any to sift through his cousin's bits and pieces. Not much had been shipped over. Johnny and Ruby had not exactly accumulated a treasure trove of memories but then, from what he had gathered, they had rented and had moved on a fairly regular basis. Souvenirs and baby photos on the mantelpiece probably hadn't been their thing.

But he should have done more than just dump the lot in the attic with the vague thought that he would go through it all on a rainy day. In his world, rainy days when you did stuff like that never happened.

'I will ensure that the oversight is rectified,' he conceded and she gave him a nod of approval.

She ordered a coffee, because he was beginning to wear the hunted expression of someone who was keen to leave, but since she had a few more things to say she would have to ensure that he stayed put, at least for a short while longer.

'When?'

'Soon.'

Ellie didn't say anything and eventually, on a note of frustration, and raking his long fingers through his hair, Luca gritted, 'Tomorrow.'

She beamed. 'Brilliant.' She looked at him and her tummy did a flip. When she was talking business, she could almost forget the impact he had on her, but as their eyes tangled she thought how gorgeous he was, how astoundingly, sinfully sexy. On the looks front, no one could deny that Luca was without comparison.

She would have to get past that if she was going to be working for him and she knew that if she could accept the magnetic pull he had over her and shrug it off then there would be no problem dealing with him.

Establishing the nature of their relationship from the outset would be a good start.

'And there's something else. I think you'll need to get more involved with Jake. Money is no substitute for time. I realise you're busy with work, but you're going to have to find the time to leave it now and again so that you can begin to build a relationship with him. He didn't run away,' she said bluntly, 'because he was so happy to be living here in London with you.'

'Anything else?' Luca asked silkily. 'Should I go on a parenting skills course to make sure I'm covering all bases?'

'Not funny.' She tilted her chin at a combative angle and outstared him. 'When I leave, it would be nice to think that you and Jake had built something a bit stronger than what's there now. He needs to really know that he's loved and wanted in order to settle properly.'

His discomfort was palpable. Luca Ross didn't do these sorts of conversations. Ellie waited, half-expecting him to shut down the dialogue and move back into his comfort zone. Instead, he said at last, 'You win. I will take some time off work.' He shook his head and shifted his piercing gaze away from her. 'I've never failed at anything in my life before and I don't intend to fail at this. I'll do what it takes.'

# CHAPTER FOUR

WITHOUT ANY FANFARE, Ellie vacated the house in which she had been renting a room. Most of the business of balancing the books was amicable and largely done over text. Rooms to rent in London which were cheap and in a relatively good location were as rare as hen's teeth and there was a list of alternative tenants—mainly friends of friends—waiting in the wings. The girls were all a pleasant bunch and they took her defection without grumbling.

Ellie didn't know whether she was relieved at the lack of fuss or saddened because she'd made so little impact, then she robustly reminded herself of the lucrative nature of her new temporary job and told herself that she would be able to afford something far better by the end of summer. A definite date hadn't been set but it would be determined by the speed with which a suitable replacement nanny was found which in turn, Ellie thought, depended on how fussy Luca intended to be. He might have given the go ahead on the last two with a casual wave of his hand but that was pre-runaway godson. Now, he had been shocked into taking stock.

She'd been bought lock, stock and barrel for the foreseeable future, and as she looked around her vacated room and reminded herself of the small fortune she would be earning over the next few weeks she couldn't prevent an uneasy shiver from running through her.

When she thought back to that conversation three days ago, she realised just how much he had controlled the outcome. He had sought her out, having done his homework, and he had baited his hook in just the right way to catch the fish he needed.

He'd known her weak spot and he had subtly but effectively played on that without appearing to be manipulative in any way—but here she was, room emptied of her possessions and stepping into waters she couldn't predict. Luca would be a fair employer but he would have impossibly high standards and she couldn't afford to let his overpowering personality suffocate her professionalism.

She knew that she would have to do more than just engage with Jake. She would have to try and build a bridge between little Jake and his older cousin. He would be cool and practical and he would expect her to be the same. She would have to squash the temptation to get hot and bothered in his presence, because if she did then all attempts to be cool and practical like him would take an instant nose dive.

Her visit to her father had been brief because, she had said, she had to return to London to start her job.

'It's quite specialist.' She had spun the truth in a way that had somehow justified the exorbitant salary she was being paid. 'This isn't just a normal situation... Jake is a very confused and mixed-up young lad...'

She was guiltily aware that in one sentence she had somehow managed to go from a primary school teacher walking dogs to a top psychologist capable of dealing with a troubled young child but, if she'd stuck rigidly to the truth, her father would have been worried sick. He wasn't an idiot. Why would someone pay over the odds for the simple job of looking after a misbehaving child? Why wouldn't he get a professional in? It would have been impossible to explain either Luca's personality, that was geared to see and take what he wanted whatever the cost, or that he had wanted her because of the peculiar nature of the situation.

Lily, she was told, was making noises about returning to England for a spell, if she could spare the time. Ellie had grimaced and concealed the bald truth that her sister had refused to contribute a penny towards paying off her father's debt.

She had had just one conversation with Luca since their dinner. She had phoned to thank him for the initial sizeable deposit of cash into her bank account and, getting to the point as he always did, he had said bluntly, 'I hope you're not getting cold feet.'

'What makes you ask that?'

'I'm good at detecting anxiety in people's voices,' he had informed her drily. 'If you're worried that you'll be working with someone you don't like, then don't be. It's immaterial whether you like me or not. You just need to respect me. The world is full of people whose values don't happen to dovetail with yours. Being an adult means training yourself not to be affected by that.'

Which had told her!

For the duration of the summer holiday, she would have to be prepared to commit fully to the job, to be there twenty-four-seven for his godson. No last-minute appointments that couldn't be broken, no dog-walking duties that had to be fulfilled and no men claiming priorities over her time.

He had asked her, at the tail end of that conversation,

and almost as an afterthought, whether there was a man in her life.

'You don't have a husband,' he had delivered in a voice that was cool and a little bored and she could picture him doing something else while he was talking to her on the phone—perhaps checking emails on his computer or reading some high-level report. 'And you don't have a live-in partner, but is there someone lurking in the background that you may have failed to mention?'

He had wanted her positioned in just the right place to suit his needs, and having anyone making demands on her time was not going to work, especially as she would be living under his roof. Considering she had only just been gaping at the sum of money in her account, she had realised in that instant just how detailed the trade between them was going to be. In short, he would call all the shots.

'As a matter of fact, I haven't at the moment.' She had stumbled over her words and her cheeks had reddened in embarrassment. Luca didn't have any interest in her personal life, except insofar as it might affect their arrangement, but she had winced with self-consciousness at the picture that admission had painted—the teacher who walked dogs, dressed in shabby clothes, with no one in her life.

Where most girls her age, with eight weeks of summer to fill, would have been booking holidays with boyfriends, she was trying to find a way to save money so that she could bail her father out of the desperate hole he had contrived to dig for himself, and there was nothing going on in her life to prevent her from doing that. She hadn't had to cancel any hot dates or rearrange any holidays with a significant other so that she could fulfil her obligations to Luca.

It had been a moment to think seriously about the direction her life had taken. She hadn't really thought about it before, but now she could see that she had thrown in the towel after her last crash-and-burn relationship. She had buried herself in her job—had breathed a sigh of relief that she hadn't actually *loved* Paul but had more been in love with the idea of being in love—and had taken the safe option of not getting involved with anyone again. She would wait for the right guy to come along.

But having to admit to Luca—sex-on-legs Luca, who had probably never spent more than a handful of nights in an empty bed—that she was resolutely single had been mortifying.

Was this where she wanted to be in a year's time? Two years' time? Okay, maybe walking dogs to earn some extra cash, but still on her own with no particular reason to look forward to the long summer holidays? Maybe getting together with a clutch of similarly single female friends so that they could go somewhere together? Was that how she had been affected by living in the shadow of her fabulously beautiful younger sister? Had she had her self-confidence sapped over the years? Even though she would always have asserted proudly that you didn't have to rely on something as superficial as looks in order to lead a brilliant and fulfilling life, had she known, somewhere deep down, that she had in all truth given up on making any effort?

When she had been dating Paul, she had made an effort. Back then, she had fussed over her appearance and done all those girly things her sister had spent a lifetime doing. She had experimented with make-up, done her nails and grown her hair, and it had all been for nothing, because he had dumped her for her sister. That had been a wake-up call for her, and after that she had promptly lost all interest in stuff that she wrote off as being superficial.

When she met someone, appearance would not make a jot of difference to how he felt about her. He wouldn't be the sort of shallow type whose head could be turned by a sexy blonde with big boobs and legs up to her armpits.

Except, she was never going to meet anyone if she didn't get out there, was she?

She was going to be living in a gilded cage for the next few weeks, and once she was back in her own world things were going to change.

Right now, the gilded cage was a joy to behold, and Ellie did a full circle of the room.

On her bed, Jake was lying in starfish mode, staring up at the ceiling, trying to think of as many things as he could that began with the letter A.

Ellie flung herself down next to him and tickled him until he started squealing for her to stop.

'Shall I tell you a secret?' she whispered, laughing, and Jake giggled.

'What?'

'This is the nicest room I've ever slept in in my entire life.'

'My room's nicer,' Jake whispered back, hugging her. 'I have a Spiderman duvet.'

'You're right,' Ellie said, in a serious hush-hush voice. 'That's the only thing that's missing and I'm going to make sure to put that right as soon as I can. No Spiderman for me, though. Maybe something princessy...'

Jake made a face and she laughed and ruffled his hair. 'Are you saying I'm not like a princess?' she teased, slip-

ping off the bed. 'Because you'd be right! I'm more like…
*the big, bad wolf* and I'm going to *gobble you up* if you
don't fly down to the kitchen this very minute and start
eating your dinner! Miss Muller called you ages ago,
you little horror!'

She might not have seen Luca since the deal had been
done, but she had seen a lot of Jake, and she could already
feel the bond between them growing.

Luca was prepared to pay the earth for her services
and she realised that this was what he wanted—this bond
between herself and his godson—because that very bond
would be the foundation for his own way in to Jake. To
put it loosely, he would use her, and for that he was willing to pay over the odds. This was the nature of their relationship and it helped to put everything in perspective.

Her settling-in period had been made even smoother
because Luca had had to go to New York on business for
the first few days after her arrival. He had kept in touch
by email and text, and spoken with her every evening
without fail to ask penetrating questions about Jake, but
she had been relieved that he wasn't around while she
found her feet.

She'd had time to relax with Jake and, bit by bit, was
finding out about his background.

The picture he was slowly painting, much to her dismay, was of a broken household with his young and irre-
sponsible parents largely absent. As he gradually opened
up, she realised that he talked more about the elderly couple in the flat next door to where he had lived, who had
obviously borne the brunt of babysitting duties when his
parents had been busy chasing the dream.

As promised, his possessions had been sorted through
while she had been visiting her father, and she had flicked

through a scant amount of photos of his parents on the laptop which had been charged up. A young, beautiful couple, largely posing against dramatic backgrounds that made the photos resemble photo shoots, with only a handful of pictures of Jake as a baby and so forth.

Little wonder that he had shrunk into himself, bewildered and confused, when he had been torn from the familiarity of his surroundings and thrust into the care of an aggressively powerful workaholic who had no patience with having his life disrupted. From the sounds of it, his life had contained precious few rules. He had attended school *sometimes* and had been allowed to do what he wanted whenever he wanted. Luca, with his authoritarian approach to life and his rigid sense of control, would have been a terrifying contrast to Jake's largely absent, easy-going, very young parents.

She would talk to Luca the following evening when he returned to London. It was going to be a two-way street and, if he thought that he could call all the shots, then he was going to be in for a surprise.

She was busy mulling over a scenario in which she could pin her demanding and arrogant employer to the spot, and force him to listen to things he would probably not want to hear, when there was a knock on her bedroom door.

Ellie answered it without thinking. Probably Jake bouncing back up for something or other.

It was Luca. For a few seconds Ellie stood and stared because she hadn't been expecting him.

She'd spent days dismissing her nonsensical response to him and now all of that flew out of the window faster than a speeding bullet as their eyes collided.

She marvelled that she had somehow forgotten how

breathtakingly *vital* Luca was, even when he needed a shave and he looked dishevelled and weary. Nothing could detract from the man's enormous sex appeal. His impact was as powerful as if she'd run headlong into a brick wall and been left dazed and disorientated.

He was in a suit but the tie had gone, as had the jacket, and he had cuffed the sleeves of his white shirt to the elbows.

She lowered her eyes, heart beating harder than a sledgehammer in her chest, and her mouth went dry, because all she could see somehow was his muscular forearms and the sprinkling of dark hair that seemed weirdly, aggressively, over-the-top *masculine*.

'What are you doing here? I thought... I wasn't ex-pecting you until tomorrow evening.'

'Things got wrapped up earlier than expected. It's not yet seven-thirty. I expected to find you downstairs.'

'I was on my way down.' She tried hard not to focus on her stunningly casual outfit—old jogging bottoms, tee shirt and bedroom slippers. These were not clothes with which she could project her professional face.

'I thought that this would be a good a time to have a face-to-face conversation before I start work. I have a hundred emails to get through but I can spare an hour or so.'

'What, now? I realise I'm being paid a lot, but that doesn't mean that you can barge into my bedroom and summon me downstairs for a chat.'

'I'm afraid it does,' Luca returned coolly.

*This was what you signed up for*, a little voice whis-pered in her head.

'I can't predict my hours,' he continued in the grow-ing silence. 'With the best will in the world, I can try and have a more reliable work schedule, but there's no guarantee that that will work out.'

'I do understand that, but I don't get why you can't arrange your schedule to accommodate Jake. You keep reminding me that you're the boss of your own company, so why can't you decide when you can leave and when you can't?'

Luca looked at her narrowly. 'I don't care for the tone of your voice.'

Back down now and cower, Ellie thought, and she would set a precedent for their relationship that would last the duration of the time she was under this roof, and it would make for a very uncomfortable situation. There would be things she would need to say to him that he would not particularly want to hear and he would need to be less of a control freak to deal with it.

'I apologise for that,' she said in a composed tone. 'And of course, I do appreciate that you can't tailor your working hours as much as you may like, but I think Jake would benefit from a predictable schedule from you, at least to start with. And that aside...' she drew in a deep breath '... I won't be disturbed any and every time you think you might want to catch up. It's not on.'

Thick, humming silence greeted this and, eventually, Luca raked his fingers through his hair and stared at her, as though debating what he should say next.

Ellie stepped into the breach and continued in a more placatory voice, 'If you give me fifteen minutes, I'll come downstairs. I just need to change.'

She used the fifteen minutes of allotted time to dress quickly into a pair of trousers and a pale blue polo shirt.

On her way down, she passed Jake, who was heading up.

'Read me a story tonight?' He looked at her and then sighed with disappointment when she told him that she couldn't.

'So you get two tomorrow night,' she promised, kneeling down and giving him an affectionate squeeze. 'Plus, Luca is back tonight. Isn't that great?' Her keen eyes noted the way his whole body tensed and he shook his head vehemently.

'Why does he have to come back?'

'Because he wants to spend some time with you.'

'I don't want to spend any time with him.'

Ellie didn't say anything. As far as mountains to climb went, this was going to be a steep one.

Ten minutes later, she was sitting at the long metal and wood table when Luca walked in; she could see he'd had a quick shower because his dark hair was still damp. He positively glistened with robust good health, an alpha male in the prime of his fitness radiating energy from every pore, and no longer looking tired.

'So.' He strolled towards the fridge and peered inside. 'Talk to me.'

Ellie gritted her teeth and wondered whether the word *polite* had ever been used to describe Luca's take on conversation.

Was he *that* short with everyone to whom he spoke? Or maybe just with the people who worked for him? Surely not? There were moments when she glimpsed such overpowering charm and charisma that she could only imagine the guy just didn't believe in wasting any of that charm or common courtesy on her because she worked for him.

And he doubly wouldn't be bothered because not only

did she work for him but she was also a *woman* and therefore would not even register on his radar.

He asked her about Jake, and she repeated a lot of what she had communicated to him via email. He was a very good listener. She could tell that he was taking in every word she was saying, and was probably working out how her activities with Jake compared to the previous two nannies.

He'd abandoned the fridge in favour of a glass of wine, and offered her a glass as a token gesture of politeness, not pressing her when she shook her head.

'I know this is going to work out,' he said when there was a pause, 'because Jake asked for you when you went to see your father.'

'He probably needed a comforting shoulder after everything he's been through. We looked at some of the photos together.' She hesitated. 'Did you go through them with him?'

'I began.' He shrugged. 'But it wasn't a success.' He didn't add that Jake had stared stonily at the ground in absolute silence, his small body stiff with tension, until Luca had flung his hands up in surrender and packed in the exercise.

'It takes time.'

'That's a commodity that's in short supply with me.' He hesitated, then added with hard-won honesty, 'I'm afraid I don't know a huge amount about children. I have no idea how to communicate with them. I don't suppose that helps.'

'You just have to be interested and genuine,' Ellie told him. 'Talk to Jake the way you would talk to…well…anyone, really. Bearing in mind he's six, so discussing world politics isn't going to get you anywhere.' She smiled and he returned it with a crooked smile of his own.

'I prefer giving orders,' Luca said. 'Or else it's down to world politics, I'm afraid.'

'You'll pick it up.' She hesitated, then explained what she had found out about Jake's background and the way he seemed to have been left to his own devices while his youthful parents had got on with their lives.

'I wouldn't say that Johnny and I were the best of friends,' Luca expanded thoughtfully. 'He was much younger and very different from me. I only met Ruby, his wife, once. At the christening. She seemed very much like him.'

'How so?'

'In love with a dream that was never going to materialise,' Luca said flatly. 'And with a baby in tow, to make matters worse. Naturally, I advised against the whole thing.'

'Naturally.'

Luca frowned. 'I'm picking something up here. What is that remark supposed to mean?'

'Being in love with a dream is just another way of saying being hopeful.'

'Which, if you don't mind me saying, is another pointless waste of time.'

Ellie wondered, in astonishment, where that depth of cynicism had stemmed from but the conversation was already over and he was standing up, restlessly prowling back to the fridge and frowning into it until she asked him, reluctantly, whether he had eaten.

'Not since yesterday,' Luca confirmed, without looking at her.

'If I had known, I would have told Miss Muller… She

stayed on later this evening because she left early yesterday. Her neighbour was poorly. She had to do some shopping for her. She prepared something for Jake and I would have—'

'Forget it. I didn't know myself that I would be returning a day early.'

'I could do something for you. Make something...'

Luca swung round to face her. 'Cooking for me isn't one of your duties,' he said flatly.

'It's no trouble,' Ellie said, standing up and making her way over to one of the cupboards, but he halted her in mid-stride, one hand on her wrist.

At that fleeting contact, a charge of electricity raced through her, sending hot sparks through her body and igniting all her nerve endings. Her nipples pinched into urgent, responsive buds and she could feel a horrifying melting between her thighs that made her want to rub her legs together. Her mouth ran dry and she stared up at him, pupils dilated, only galvanising her treacherous body into action when he removed his hand and stood back to stare at her narrowly.

Dismayed that she might have revealed far more than she wanted to, Ellie stepped back, but her heart was thundering and her skin was hot and prickly.

It didn't matter how much she told herself that she needed to be businesslike and efficient, she couldn't seem to help the way her body reacted when it was around him.

She had never suffered that sort of weakness before and she was baffled as to how she could suffer it now with a man who, however drop-dead gorgeous he was, did not appeal to her on any other level at all.

'No.' Luca pinned his fabulous dark eyes on her flushed face as he helped himself to bread and unearthed some cheese from the fridge. He didn't bother with butter or anything else. 'Like I told you, cooking for me isn't part of the deal, and I won't have it.'

'Right.'

'You're offended,' he said shortly, sitting down and then relaxing back to look at her with brooding intensity while she hovered in the middle of the sprawling kitchen like a fish out of water, wanting desperately to leave, but knowing that she would have to be formally dismissed before she could do so.

'Why should I be? Of course I'm not. I was merely being polite. Of course I know that cooking for you isn't part of the deal.'

'I don't do *women cooking for me*,' Luca told her, releasing her from the suffocating stranglehold of his stare and eating the bread and cheese without enthusiasm. 'I don't like it, and I never encourage it, so there's no need to feel piqued because I turned down your offer.'

'I told you, I don't,' Ellie said stiffly. It was now fair to assume that she wasn't going to be dismissed just yet so she sidled across to the chair facing him and sank into it with relief. 'And, while we're on the subject of deals, you've spent the past couple of days abroad and after this you're off to work. Maybe you should look in on Jake? Say goodnight? I'm sure he'd really appreciate that.' She crossed her fingers at the little white lie. Horror would be a more predictable reaction from Jake if Luca were to show up on a godfather-godson bonding mission.

'I...' Luca looked at her and, for a moment, she saw someone who might be top of the food chain when it came to making money, but who when it came to the relationship with his godson was touchingly vulnerable.

'He's probably asleep,' she said quickly. 'You wouldn't want to wake him.'

Luca nodded briskly. The whole thing was a bloody nightmare and he was only now really appreciating the extent of it because he was being called upon to interact instead of throwing money at the problem and leaving it to the professionals. He'd sworn to himself that this was a challenge he would overcome, but how equipped was he to handle the demands of a screwed-up kid?

*Highly equipped*, a little voice inside him whispered.

Introspection had never played a part in his life. Luca was someone who powered through, eyes firmly set on the present and the future, because nothing about the past could be changed so why dwell on it? He particularly didn't dwell on his emotional past, which had always been better secured under lock and key, but he unlocked that place now.

His background was, on the surface, so different from Jake's. He had known happiness right up to the point when his mother had died. After that, his father had retreated behind impenetrable walls and, when he had, he had taken Luca's childhood with him, leaving behind a young boy forced to grow up fast and to find his independence at an age when he should still have been playing with toy cars and Action Man heroes. All the money in the world had not been able to compensate for the absence of his father.

Had that been a childhood? Yes, he had certainly learnt to thank his years spent at that boarding school for providing him with the sort of backbone that could win any fight. But could you have called it a *childhood*?

You didn't have to be a genius to work out that Jake

would tread a predictable path if Luca didn't get his hands dirty and engage with the situation.

'I'm glad you're here,' he said gruffly. He stood up and she followed suit.

She smiled and he moved towards her, his expression unusually hesitant.

When she looked up, he was so close to her that her heart seemed to skip a beat.

He reached out. She wasn't even sure whether he was aware he was doing anything but what he did was devastating. He brushed her cheek with his finger. A soft, brief gesture that was there and gone in a heartbeat.

'And if I don't tell you that,' he finished awkwardly, 'it's not because I don't think it.'

The moment was gone but her heart was still thumping long after he'd disappeared off to work.

# CHAPTER FIVE

'THINKING OF COMING HOME? When?' Ellie was having this rushed conversation on the phone to her father whilst keeping one eye on the front door.

The past week had been a busy one. At the start of this job, she had been determined to keep some distance and to remember that she was doing this purely for the money. She wasn't in it to build a lasting relationship with Jake, far less his complicated godfather.

Unfortunately, she had felt herself being sucked into the family dynamic as the week progressed. Luca had made big efforts to keep to his side of the bargain, to put in more of an appearance than he had previously.

Jake had tolerated his presence. One step forward, two steps back. She had watched and noted Luca's frustration, for once playing a game the rules of which he hadn't made and didn't get.

She had tried to limit her interventions, but they had both turned to her variously to mediate their awkward interaction, where neither side seemed to know quite what to do.

Luca, on the back foot, was not the arrogant guy she had so disliked on first sight.

Jake, tiptoeing around like a shy deer hoping to sneak

past a predator to get to a stream, was increasingly working his way into her heart.

'Not giving a date yet,' she heard her father say with pleasure in his voice. 'She'll be busy over there. Said she can snatch a week or so to return. Can't spare longer than that. Something about agents hounding her.'

'Well, that's nice anyway.' Ellie wondered whether the little chat she had had with her sister a couple of weeks ago had galvanised her into doing something to check up on their father. She hoped so. It was no longer important whether Lily contributed to the financial situation because that was, miraculously, in hand but she knew that her father would be thrilled to have his youngest daughter come and visit.

'Told her you weren't going to be around much to come up here and visit,' her father continued. 'Told her you were hard at it in London, sorting out that little lad.'

'Yes, indeed,' Ellie mumbled guiltily.

'She'll want to see you, Els. She specifically mentioned how keen she was to meet up. Think she might be impressed by what you're doing.'

Ellie couldn't see that herself because Lily had never been particularly impressed by anything that hadn't involved being in the public eye and preferably surrounded by adoring admirers. So why was she suddenly interested in a job that involved looking after a child? But Ellie swallowed back a tart reply while manoeuvring to conclude the conversation.

This evening she would be going out with Luca, leaving Jake with a babysitter who lived three doors down.

This was about business. It was a perfect opportunity to broaden Jake's horizons when it came to interaction with other adults on the home front. They would be discussing progress. There was a script to be obeyed and Ellie was going to make sure she stuck to it.

But she hadn't stopped thinking about the way he had oh-so-casually touched her. She'd been set alight and, deep inside, there remained something smouldering, waiting to re-ignite.

For a few seconds, their eyes had met, and she had felt *something* stir between them, something hot and dangerous, but it had been over in the blink of an eye. It preyed on her mind, though, that brief connection.

It was a relief, in a way, that he had made sure to keep everything between them businesslike since then. They had semi-formal discussions in his office, employer and employee discussing work-related matters. She sat opposite him, perched forward, hands on her lap, and reported on the day's events, and stopped short of actually submitting a written report only by a whisker.

Tonight, though, it would be an experiment in getting Jake accustomed to a change of face. It had been Ellie's idea, because there was no point in allowing Jake to settle into such a comfort zone that any new person on the scene would be viewed, once again, with suspicion and mistrust.

She had suggested the young girl a few houses away because the girl owned a dog and they had chatted briefly on a couple of occasions. She had visited the girl's parents and satisfied herself that she was an excellent babysitting option.

Ellie had imagined the girl popping over to babysit during the day, even if Ellie remained upstairs in her suite catching up on work prep for the forthcoming term. She hadn't foreseen an evening out with Luca, but here she was.

She was alarmed at the level of excitement racing through her, touching all her nerve endings like little electric charges pulsing through every pore of her body. The minute the lines between employer and employee were even a tiny bit blurred, Ellie found that she was frighteningly far from immune to his raw, animal sex appeal which he exuded in punishing waves without even having to try. She had caught herself looking at him— sidelong, surreptitious glances that felt like the stolen glances of a lover. When she was within a metre of him, she could feel the heat of his body as though she was standing too close to an open flame—and the only saving grace was the fact that talking about Jake was a constant reminder that she was in paid employ.

Tonight, though…a meal out.

She had debated whether to wear her parents' meeting outfit of neat skirt, responsible, worker-bee blouse tucked into the waistband and her no-nonsense pumps, but on the spur of the moment she'd opted for something less formal because it was a lovely summer evening.

She had treated herself to a couple of summer dresses and she looked at her reflection in the mirror now. She didn't have the curves of a lingerie model but she looked okay.

The colour suited her dark colouring. It was a pale bronze and made her look ever so faintly exotic. The dress was short and skimmed her slender body lovingly and the shoes, with a little heel, did great things for her bare, brown legs. She'd also made the most of her eyes which she had always considered her best feature.

This wasn't a date and *she knew that*, but why shouldn't she wear what any other twenty-something would wear if she happened to be going out for a meal?

She would have worn this very outfit, she thought, running lightly down the stairs towards the kitchen where Luca had told her he'd be waiting, if she'd been going out with a bunch of girlfriends. No big deal.

She entered the kitchen unhurriedly and took a few deep breaths as Luca, who had been absently gazing through the kitchen window, slowly turned to face her.

He was tugging at his tie, loosening it, and for a few seconds he stilled.

'You're on time. Good.' Luca had perfected the art of glancing at Ellie without really taking her in fully. His reaction to her—one that continually caught him off-guard, the tug she induced in his groin—was unwelcome, inappropriate and incomprehensible because she wasn't his type at all. Too slight, too fierce, too outspoken and too flat-chested.

He had gone out of his way to underline their working relationship. No casual chatting in the kitchen, which would smell of something more intimate than he wanted. In the formal sitting room, they interacted in the way an employer interacted with someone he happened to be interviewing for a job.

He didn't get why she affected his libido the way she did, but he was working overtime to control his wayward response. That one and only moment, when he had given in to the urge to touch her, had galvanised his body into a reaction that had shocked him in its intensity. Her skin had been as smooth as satin under his fingers. He had had to fight down the urge to slip a finger into her mouth, feel her suck it then tug her close to lose himself in her sweetness.

Now, though…

There was no need for this so-called meeting to be conducted at night, nor was it necessary for the venue to be an expensive country pub. Lunch at the noisy local wine bar would have sufficed, but his rational brain had decided to take a break when that choice had been made.

He lowered his eyes, lashes concealing his expression, but he didn't have to stare at her because the image was imprinted in his head. She was in a dress that hugged her slender body and accentuated her ballerina grace. Her breasts were pert and rounded. Her legs were tanned, slim and shapely, and the shortness of her dark hair emphasised the contours of her delicate face and the swan-like grace of her neck.

'I usually am,' she responded quickly, heart picking up speed as she tried and failed not to look at him. 'Last time, there was a reason I was a little late.'

'I believe you. You're not one of these women who shows up late to prove a point or stage a grand entrance.'

Ellie sensed that this was one of those vaguely offensive remarks loosely gift-wrapped as a compliment of sorts.

Old feelings of insecurity rose to the surface like scum. She'd thought she'd put those feelings to rest. Living in her sister's shadow, knowing that she was the plain Jane with the brains, had been tough, especially because their mother had made no attempt to disguise her preference for Lily. But it was only now, in the company of Luca, that she realised just how deeply old wounds could cut.

Luca was so imperfect when it came to every single thing Ellie used as a benchmark for men. Yes, she had had glimpses of someone so much more complex than he appeared on first sight, but the truth was that he was still a billionaire with all the traits of a billionaire. Arrogant, ruthless, intolerant of imperfections, uncompromising. Faced with the arrival of his little charge, he had made no concessions until Jake had absconded, at which point he had got his act together. To some extent. If Jake had never run away, God only knew how much interaction he would have had with his forbidding and powerful god-father, the man from whom he was destined to inherit a multi-billion-euro business. None, Ellie suspected.

All those downsides and yet… Luca was so physically perfect a specimen. So sinfully sexy. Once she started looking at him, she couldn't seem to tear her eyes away, and her brain went into hibernation, leaving her at the mercy of all sorts of confusing, unwelcome reactions.

Ellie knew that she could keep at the forefront of her mind the fact that Luca was the sort of guy who would always be attracted to leggy blondes like Lily. It was galling that she was attracted to him. She could blame her hormones, and tell herself that he *was* ridiculously attractive, so it was no wonder she found him so, but none of that counted for anything. He wasn't her type, so why did she find him so compelling?

The way he was looking at her, his dark, intelligent eyes shielding all expression, made her wonder what was going through his head. Was he amused because she had dressed up? Did he think that she might be getting ideas into her head and maybe thinking that this was some kind of date instead of just an alternative venue for their usual daily debrief about his godson? Maybe he thought she hadn't taken the hint when he'd begun conducting their brief meetings in the more formal sitting room.

'I don't do grand entrances and I'm almost always on time,' Ellie said, grinding her teeth together, because that was just the sort of prissy statement that a truly boring person would come out with. 'It...it goes with the job.'

'Goes with the job?'

'When you teach, there isn't an option to swan in and out of class at whatever time happens to take your fancy. You have to get in at a certain time and it's a habit that's become ingrained. It's not the sexiest trait in the world, but there you go.'

Ellie went bright red and averted her eyes as he smiled slowly and walked towards her.

'I like it,' Luca told her honestly. 'It's a fallacy that men enjoy being kept waiting because a woman needs five hours to apply some war paint. Speaking of which...' He paused, and in that pause Ellie could feel herself tingling all over and waiting for him to *do something*. He had that look in his eyes. The dark depths were lazy and slumberous. He was so close to her, so close that she could feel the warmth of his body heat radiating and enveloping her. 'We should be heading off...'

Ellie blinked. He was still looking down at her. Her throat was parched but she managed to croak, 'Where are we going?'

'I thought we'd get out of London.' For once, he left the driver behind and she followed him to the garage where his Maserati was housed. He opened the passenger door for her and she slid inside a car that smelled of leather and walnut and breathed shameless luxury.

He turned to her just as he switched on the engine which roared into life. 'Forty minutes and we can sample the joys of a country pub. I don't do rural, but I also don't get many opportunities to take this car out, so why not?'

He drove with the skill and confidence of someone comfortable behind the wheel of a fast, powerful car. In between talking about Jake and the advances she was see-ing in him, Ellie let herself linger on the flex of his mus-cled forearm as he changed gears, and the lean beauty of his profile as he stared ahead, concentrating on the road and listening to every word she was saying.

'It's taking longer than I thought,' he mused.

'What is?'

'Relationship building.' Luca shot her a sideways glance.

'It's not an overnight process.' Ellie stared ahead as they left the busy hustle of London and began cruising out towards Oxford. 'Think of your own childhood,' she urged, 'and how complex the relationship you had with your parents was. It's all about having the trust there so that you're free to make mistakes, on either side, know-ing it's not going to affect the balance of the relationship. In this case it's made all the more complicated because of the situation.'

'I can't really fall back on personal experience, as I may have mentioned,' Luca said drily. 'Please don't paint rosy images of me as a kid. I was sent to boarding school when I was quite young after my mother died. My rela-tionship with my father was, in actual fact, a very simple one. He paid the school fees.'

'You're so…*matter of fact* about it,' she observed, drawn to the tight line of his lips, the expression of some-one who had few touching memories when it came to his past.

'Where's the point in getting worked up over a past that can't be changed? You work in a tough school. You must have encountered kids with more pressing problems than an eight-year-old from a rich background who ends up in a boarding school.'

'I guess that's one way of looking at it,' she said slowly. But the way he had bluntly stated those facts...*mother dying, boarding school, absentee father...and eight years old!* Somehow the situation in Luca's case felt quite different from Jake's insofar as there were alternative parental choices that could have been made. Luca's father had still been around but instead of reaching out he had chosen to walk away.

'You *would* find it difficult to bond if you...er—'

'Let's drop the Good Samaritan take on this. Bottom line is that we need to speed the process up,' he interrupted her. 'Jake is with the neighbour this evening, but sooner or later the hunt for a nanny has to commence, and by the time it concludes he should feel more confident in my relationship with him to make for a happier home environment.'

'Speed it up? How do you intend to do that?' That glimpse of humanity underneath the icy exterior was as fleeting as those other glimpses of him that showed her a man who was not the intimidating powerhouse he projected to the outside world, but it touched her in ways she couldn't explain. She pictured a bewildered child, holding back his grief as he was dispatched into the care of efficient strangers. No wonder he found it impossible to bond with his nephew. He had no experience of family life to fall back on. For all the ups and downs within her own family, who had been far from perfect, she at least had known the ebb and flow of how families operated.

'You're the touchy-feely one with the people skills,' Luca told her flatly. 'You should have one or two ideas. Here's the thing—with the best will in the world, time isn't on my side. You need to busy yourself thinking about how we solve this problem. Anyway, we're here.'

Ellie realised that they had either been driving longer than she'd thought or faster than she'd imagined because they were now in a very civilised part of the world. The houses were all set back from the road and dotted in between fields. Only the distant sound of the motorway served as a reminder that they weren't in the deepest countryside.

The pub was a chocolate box concoction of old beams, cream walls and a sprawling courtyard in which were lined up high-end cars interspersed with a couple of motorbikes.

It was still warm, even though the sun was no longer high in the sky, and the garden at the back was packed, with only a couple of free tables, one of which Luca took, settling her before returning with a bar menu and a bottle of wine.

'My driver can get here and return to London in the Maserati.' He poured them both a glass of wine. 'And we can take a taxi back to London. Now, let's talk ways forward with Jake.'

'I don't know how you think I can work miracles and suddenly speed up his recovery process and cement the relationship you two have.' She frowned and stared off into the distance, seeing but not really noticing the crowd of expensive-looking people filling out the place. She rested her eyes on his cool, beautiful face. 'You may think that you don't need to have any input into trying to find a solution to this, that so long as you unbend enough to get back from work a little earlier than you're accustomed to doing, it's enough, but you're wrong. You won't thank me for saying this, but throwing money at the situation isn't going to work the way it may have done for you when you were a child.'

Ellie didn't mean a word of that. Personally, Luca's cold, unemotional take on the world was probably directly related to the way his father had dealt with the situation and no one could say that the end result had been a blazing success, even if the guy was as rich as Croesus.

She looked at the uncompromising, unwelcoming lines of his lean, striking face and had an insane desire to reach out and stroke his cheek, the same way he had casually reached out and stroked hers. His boundaries were steel-clad and she wondered whether anyone had ever come close to breaching them. Any of those women he had dated? She thought not. He would never allow any of them near enough.

'Don't get me wrong…'

'No need to butter me up before you drop the axe.' Luca grinned because, against all odds, he was amused by the uncomfortable tinge of colour in her cheeks. 'You have amazing eyes,' he murmured, in a voice that implied that he was as surprised by what he had just said as she was.

'I beg your pardon?'

'It's an unusual shade of green, as clear as glass washed up on a beach.'

Ellie could feel herself burning up under his lazy, dark eyes. 'I… I don't think that's…appropriate, do you?'

'Possibly not,' Luca murmured. His eyes drifted to her mouth, full lips the colour of crushed raspberries and made for kissing.

'Stop looking at me,' Ellie whispered, breaking the silence with difficulty.

'You don't like it?'

'No, I most certainly do not!'

Luca raised his eyebrows and smiled and she wondered whether he thought that she might actually *like* him staring at her. She'd never played with fire and this felt as though she had a box of matches in one hand and a tank of petrol in the other. It wasn't a game she cared to begin.

'You need to spend a bit more undiluted time with Jake.' Back to the reason they were sitting here! 'I think that might be the way to go if you want to speed things up. Half an hour in the evening is better than what you were putting in before but it's not nearly enough.'

He surfaced to something she was saying and realised that he'd dropped the ball for a minute there because he'd been too busy looking at her. *Spend more time.* Time was money for him, but he was being pinned into a corner, and somehow his brain wasn't functioning at optimum level.

He heard the voice and recognised it almost before he registered that he was being addressed.

Heidi Troon had been his last girlfriend and she had not accepted the parting of ways with philosophical equanimity. She had screeched and squawked and accused him of leading her on, then she had wept and wailed and finally, in the absence of a suitable response, she had flounced out of his apartment, having called him every unladylike name under the sun and swearing darkly that he would get what was coming to him. That had been some months previously and since then her vitriolic departure, along with a certain boredom with the prospect of wooing a replacement, had propelled Luca into increasing his workload. Jake, in retrospect, had not been a happy beneficiary of the situation.

He turned around with visible reluctance as she arrived at his side, her big blue eyes staring at Ellie with open curiosity before zeroing in on him.

This was a woman designed to make men swoon and bump into lamp posts. With legs up to her armpits and hair that fell in a golden sheet to her waist, she knew how to play up every single asset she possessed to perfection, and her assets were many.

She was wearing a small red skirt and a small, cropped black-and-white sleeveless top that clung to every curve, and the striking length of her legs was accentuated by six-inch strappy sandals.

'I've been trying to get in touch with you,' she crooned and Luca gritted his teeth. 'We left on bad terms and afterwards, well, I thought I could make it up to you. I've phoned and texted…'

'I know.'

'Why haven't you replied?'

'I've been busy. Heidi…this is Ellie.'

Ellie had never seen anyone as stupendous as the blonde towering over their table. She wasn't sure whether to stand, sit, smile, stretch out her hand or explain why she was sitting in a country pub with Luca. Or maybe just curtsy. She opted for the path of least resistance and looked away in silence, leaving Luca to deal with the situation.

'I wanted to talk to you, Luca. Without your…*who are you anyway?*…earwigging.'

Luca sighed and stood up, his lean, handsome face tight with disapproval. 'I'll be back shortly,' he grated, while Ellie grinned like a wind-up toy until her jaw ached.

Hot embarrassment was coursing through her. Had she been lulled into thinking that this was *a date*? Well, she'd been brought right back down to earth with a bump, and let that be a lesson to her.

By the time Luca returned, the blonde was no longer with him, and Ellie was halfway through her food.

'Apologies,' she said stiffly.

'For what?'

'For getting in the way if you would rather have dined with your friend.'

'If I'd wanted the woman around, I would have asked her to stay. I didn't ask her to stay because the last thing I wanted was her company.'

'She must have been curious about me. What did you tell her?'

'Nothing.' His expression was cool and unrevealing. 'Why would I tell her anything? It's none of her business.' He shrugged and said, by way of brief explanation, 'We went out some time ago. It didn't last long but she took the break-up badly, even though I'd been nothing but honest with her from day one. She has been trying to contact me and I've been ignoring her texts. I had said what had to be said and that, as far as I was concerned, was the end of the story. My apologies if you felt uncomfortable with the situation.'

'Not at all,' Ellie lied. 'But don't you care if she gets the wrong impression?'

'Wrong impression?' Amusement lightened his features. 'Ah, I get where you're going with this. I repeat: what she thinks is her concern. I can't legislate over her thoughts and I have never seen the need to explain myself to anyone.' That *had* occurred to him, and he'd thought, so what if she thought that Ellie was her replacement? Wouldn't it stop her thinking that there was still a chance for them and bring an end to the nuisance calls? Why would he shut down that line of thought when it was beneficial to him that she run with the misconception?

'Has it occurred to you that *I* might care what some-one else thinks of me?'

'No,' Luca answered truthfully. 'You don't know the woman so why would you care what she thinks of you? You'll never see her again and, if she chooses to gossip a bit with her crowd, then it won't make a scrap of dif-ference to you because you'll never know.'

Everything he said made sense, but Ellie was still dis-mayed at the thought of having her reputation used as gossip fodder for people like the stalking blonde. Being seen with Luca, being thought of as the latest in his line of mistresses, did not sit well with her. She had noticed the way the other woman had looked at her with those icy blue eyes—with pitying speculation.

'Don't think about it,' he said dismissively. 'If you worried about what everyone thinks, you'd go mad.'

'Thanks for the tip,' Ellie muttered, lowering her eyes and half-wanting to slap him, because maybe that was how it worked in his world, but it wasn't how it worked in hers. Plus, somehow the atmosphere had been ruined, and while she knew that there should have been no at-mosphere to ruin in the first place she still felt flat all of a sudden.

'You're welcome,' Luca drawled. 'You'll thank me for it one day, even though right now you look as though you'd ram your foot on the accelerator and run me over if you happened to be behind the wheel of a truck.'

'Not everyone sees the world the way you do.' Ellie looked at him defensively but he had obviously put that moment of unpleasantness behind him and was already half-smiling at her.

'What a shame.' The smile turned into a grin. Her breathing hitched, and some of that determination to remind herself that this was *business and not pleasure* was chipped away. 'Now, moving on, there was something I wanted to discuss with you before that untimely interruption. You say that I need more time with my godson and I happen to agree with you. The only way I can think of doing that is to remove myself from the office altogether.'

'What does that mean?'

'Take time off. Two weeks. I won't be able to fully escape the workload, but there will be considerably fewer demands on my attention. I own a villa in Majorca. I can't remember the last time I went there and I'm thinking that this would be a good opportunity to pay it a visit. Naturally you would have to come along.'

'Two weeks? Out of the country?' Ellie was thinking *sun, sea, sand...and Luca. What kind of a mix was that?*

'You'll find that it will be a luxurious two-week holiday. Yes, it'll be a busman's holiday insofar as your interaction with Jake is concerned, but I can guarantee relaxation. The villa is a short walk down to a private cove. When we return to London, the hunt for your replacement can begin in earnest, and I'm hoping that some undiluted time with Jake will build more of a bridge between us than currently exists.'

'When would we leave? I had hoped to go up north next weekend. My sister is planning on coming over and seems keen to meet up...'

'I should be able to tie up all loose ends and get my calendar cleared within three days. Aim for that. The sister can be put on hold. Three days should give you time to buy whatever you want to take with you in terms of summer clothes, as well as whatever Jake needs. It'll be hot out there. Questions?'

None, Ellie thought, as her life hurtled into fifth gear

and the predictability which had been the mainstay of her existence threatened to vanish altogether. She'd taken his deal and signed her soul away in the process. So how could she have any questions?

And then, at five the following evening, questions became redundant anyway because fate decided to speed things along. In the kitchen with Jake, Ellie was startled by the sound of the front door slamming and then, seconds later, Luca strode into the kitchen, face as black as thunder.

He tossed two tabloids on the table and said, before Ellie could recover from her astonishment at seeing him, 'Turn to the gossip column. Jake.' He spun to look at his godson. 'Exciting news. We're going on a trip. Find Miss Muller and start packing whatever you want to take with you. Ellie will be up in a minute.'

'We bought some Lego. Can I take it?' Jake hovered, nervous eyes locking on Ellie.

'Whatever you want.' Then Luca seemed to think about it because he knelt to Jake's level and said, tone slightly softened, 'But there will be a lot to do out there. A pool, the sea... There's even a boat.'

'A boat?' Jake's eyes lit up and, for the first time, Ellie could see real interest there in what Luca was saying just as she could see the effort Luca was making to remember that he was dealing with a six-year-old child and so had to exercise patience.

'Nothing fancy, but you don't need fancy to do a bit of sailing.'

'Will you teach me how to sail?'

'I could do that.'

Luca smiled and Ellie felt a lump form in her throat.

Something inside her bubbled up, something quite different from the fierce sexual awareness that gripped her whenever she was in his presence.

The way he was now with Jake—a certain softness in his manner, as though he was deliberately slowing himself down—touched her.

Then, Jake gone, things were back to normal and Luca was focusing on Ellie, striding forward to help himself to some water while he tugged off his tie with one hand and flung it on the table. 'It seems that my ex has had a little mischief at our expense. You're the newest acquisition in my long and chequered line of women.'

The colour drained from Ellie's face. She snatched up the paper and there, in bold print, were riveting revelations about a non-existent relationship which, Heidi had made sure to reveal, could really be serious because, for once, the most eligible man on the planet was not dating to type.

'I'm even more furious than you are,' Luca said with audible loathing in his voice.

'You have to tell these reporters that none of this is true!' Ellie was horrified at what her dad would think. He would be bitterly disappointed. She had never been the type of girl to sleep around and get herself emblazoned in tabloid papers. He might never find out, but Lily was going to be around, and she read tabloids as thoroughly as a student cramming for an end-of-year exam.

'I don't discuss my private life with reporters,' Luca informed her, his movements restless and lacking their usual grace. 'And for the record, never get into a dialogue with the paparazzi unless you want every word misconstrued.'

'So what do you suggest? You might not care about any of this but *I do*!'

'It'll be a five-minute wonder. You can tell your father the truth but that isn't going to make the article disappear. There will be reporters trying to take pictures of you out and about and embellishing a non-story as much as they can until some other nonsense comes along to distract them.'

'Pictures of me?' Ellie squeaked, paling at the thought of that intrusion into her privacy.

'Not if we leave the country. I have my private jet on standby. You just need to pack your bags and I'll ensure we leave this house without being followed. My villa is more secure than the Bank of England and, by the time we return, all of this will have blown over.' He glanced at his watch, dumped his empty glass in the sink and looked at her. 'I will see you in the hallway in an hour, Ellie.' Then unexpectedly his voice was gentle when he added, 'I realise I have a different take on this to you, Ellie, but everything will be fine in the end. You just have to trust me on this…'

# CHAPTER SIX

WITHIN AN HOUR and a half, they were being driven in his Jag out to the airstrip where his private jet would be ready and waiting for them. There were no reporters in sight, but there were two black Range Rovers driving behind them at a discreet distance, and they had been ushered out of the house via a side door straight into a waiting chauffeur-driven car.

She hadn't managed to cobble anything together by way of summer clothes, so her case was full of the stuff she wore every day. Jeans and tee shirts. A couple of pairs of shorts and some flip-flops. Jake, fortunately, had an ample supply of designer summer gear, which had been provided along with all the expensive trinkets and gadgets that Luca had ordered in for him as a replacement for *quality time*.

The sun was fading by the time they made it to the airstrip which was forty minutes outside London. In the car, Luca worked and Jake stared excitedly out of the window before asking repeatedly when they were going to be there, and Ellie...

Ellie marvelled that her well-ordered, neat little life had detonated without her even realising that there had been a hand grenade waiting to go off.

This was an adventure, and it felt like one. Except she didn't do adventures. Her sister did. Which, for most of the silent drive, brought her right back to the business of her father and hoping he didn't read all the rubbish that had been circulating in the tabloids...

The private jet—which clearly Luca took for granted, as he barely glanced at it—was amazing.

Sleek, black and powerful, bearing the logo of his company in dull, matt silver along the side, it oozed crazy wealth and Jake was so impressed that he sidled closer to Luca, who had paused to look down at his godson.

The promise of a sailing lesson had opened a crack in the door between them, even if neither of them was quite aware of that, and Ellie took a back seat, allowing them both awkwardly to try their hand at communicating without her intervention.

Jake asked questions about the jet and Luca broke down his answers into bite-sized replies, easily digested by a curious six-year-old.

'Perhaps you could teach me how to fly?' Jake asked as they boarded, and Luca burst out laughing.

'That might have to wait,' he said, looking down as Jake strapped himself in. 'A pilot's licence is the one thing I haven't yet had time to get. But don't worry. You want to fly my jet? You'll get the chance in time.'

'Wow,' Ellie murmured with heartfelt sincerity when Luca was sitting next to her, while behind them Jake occupied himself with something on his tablet. 'I think you're working out how this whole father-son thing works...' Then she blushed and clumsily amended, 'I meant godfather-godson.'

'Stick to the former.' Luca pulled out his laptop, eyes

not on her. 'It's more appropriate considering he will inherit the throne.'

'Inherit the throne?'

'What I have will one day be his.' He looked at her thoughtfully. 'I would like to have a meaningful relationship with the child who will, one day, take over my empire.'

'More than the relationship you have with your own father,' Ellie heard herself say, but instead of slamming down the shutters hard Luca nodded abruptly.

'Something like that.' He stared at her for a few seconds, then adjusted his position and murmured softly, 'And, Ellie, don't think about what other people are going to say or how they're going to react to a couple of trashy articles printed in some tabloids. I can see it's on your mind. Don't focus on it.'

She nodded but didn't answer as the jet began taxiing for take-off. It thundered into the heavens with the power of a rocket and she couldn't contain a gasp of excitement, which took her mind off the whole sorry business for a couple of minutes.

'Did you get through to your father?' Luca asked as soon as they were airborne.

'No,' Ellie told him glumly.

'It's more than likely he won't read those articles. Is he the sort who has a penchant for trashy tabloids?'

'One of them isn't a trashy tabloid.' Her green eyes were filled with anxiety. He lived in such a different world from her, she thought again. He occupied a world where he was such a top dog that other people's opinions didn't matter and he had complete freedom to do exactly what he wanted. Looking at him was like looking at an alien from another planet.

'You're getting lost in the details.' Luca smiled. Her worry was palpable. He should have been irritated because he disliked hand-holding, especially when it came to situations where the hand-holding concerned something he personally considered trivial, but he wasn't irritated. In fact, he wanted to smooth away her anxiety. He felt a tightening in his groin as his gaze dropped to her full mouth and he breathed slowly and deeply, regaining control. It would help if she wasn't staring at him with eyes that could have melted ice.

'It's a storm in a tea cup. Trust me on this one. The paparazzi are fickle. I might be marginally newsworthy but I'm a businessman, not a celebrity. The only reason they've picked up on this at all is because I'm rich and because Heidi is a model who enjoys getting her name and face out there. Reporters love her and she knows just how to throw mud around.'

'Your storm in a tea cup is my personal nightmare,' Ellie said, worrying her lower lip and then leaning back against the leather seat to close her eyes briefly. 'And even if my father doesn't read tabloids, which he doesn't, my sister devours them, and she'll be reporting the incident in great detail.'

'Ah, your sister, the one who has so much in common with me. I recall you saying something of the sort.'

Ellie shrugged one narrow shoulder and kept her profile averted. She didn't want to talk about Lily. She didn't want him to be curious about her sister. Why was that? she wondered. It wasn't as though they were ever going to cross paths. She hated the thought of that happening but refused to analyse why.

'I'll try and take it all in my stride,' she said, eyes still closed, which made this awkward conversation a lot easier. 'But I don't live in your world where this kind of thing happens. You're used to dealing with it, and besides, you don't really care what people think anyway. We're chalk and cheese.'

'I won't argue with that.'

'That's why this whole situation is so stupid,' she thought aloud.

'Why?'

'Because...' Ellie turned to him then drew back a little because it felt as if he was way closer to her than she'd thought. She could smell the clean, woody scent of whatever aftershave he used and could see the tawny glitter in the dark depths of his eyes. 'Because anyone would take one look at us and know that there was no way we could be anything other than employer and employee.'

'You don't do justice to yourself,' Luca said softly. 'What makes you think I don't find you sexy?'

Ellie's eyes widened and then she said, angrily, 'Please don't think you have to compliment me to make me feel good about myself. I feel very good about myself. I'm just realistic.'

'Look in the mirror, Ellie.' Luca's voice was mild and unrevealing.

Ellie's head was swimming. She couldn't maintain eye contact. What was he saying? That he found her *attractive*? She refused to believe it. She had seen his last girlfriend and she was nothing like her.

If she had looked like Lily, well, that would have been a different matter.

Ellie hated all the old insecurities that had somehow been revived ever since she had met Luca. She didn't understand why that was so and it was frustrating that those insecurities were pursuing her so doggedly when she thought she'd left all that behind a long time ago. Was it because he was the sort of beautiful person she had trained herself to ignore over the years? She'd hunkered down after the boyfriend that never was. She knew the limits of her sexual appeal and was very content to work with what she had. But Luca's compliments? Why should he be allowed to feel sorry for her?

'I look in the mirror every day,' she said crisply, 'and I'm not exactly a six-foot blonde whose best friends are reporters and who enjoys having her face splashed across gossip columns in tabloid newspapers, am I?'

'No, you're definitely not that.'

'And thank goodness for that!' Ellie was stung by his easy acceptance of what she had said.

'But as my ex made clear in that article, what about the theory that opposites attract?'

Ellie laughed shortly. 'I don't think so.' She was beginning to squirm because the conversation seemed to be meandering down all sorts of unpredictable roads and, the more it meandered, the more out of control she was beginning to feel. 'Men always go for the same types.'

'Is that your personal observation?'

'As a matter of fact, it is,' Ellie said coolly. Their eyes tangled and she powered on, determined not to be the first to look away. 'Not,' she added gamely, 'that my private life is any of your business.'

'No, of course it isn't,' Luca murmured, his interest piqued in ways that took him by surprise. 'And I won't muddy the waters by pretending that it is. Although...'

'Although what?' The lengthening silence threatened to wreak havoc with her fragile composure.

Ellie hadn't had much choice when it had come to this arrangement. In fact, she'd had *zero* choice. For the amount of money he was paying her, she would have been obliged to follow him to Timbuktu for the job, had she been asked. In the absence of any choice, she had tried not to give house room to the tricky technicality of what it would feel like being cooped up with him all day for hours on end with very little reprieve.

Trepidation soared inside her as he continued to look at her with lazy, brooding intensity, his dark eyes so unsettling and so compelling.

'We're going to be in one another's company for longer periods of time than we have been so far.'

'Yes, I realise that, but I'm here for Jake, and I suppose it's no different than if you were to go somewhere on business with your secretary.'

'Very, very different,' Luca corrected without batting an eyelid. 'I've never shared a villa with my secretary before. Not to mention the fact that the business of Jake takes this to a very personal level.'

'Perhaps *personal* is the wrong word.'

Luca shrugged. 'My point is that there's a limit to how formal things are going to be once we get to the villa. I feel it's only fair to warn you of that in case you're beginning to feel nervous about the situation.'

'Thank you for that,' Ellie said politely, eyes sliding away from this dark, beautiful face.

The jet began dipping and she jumped up to check on Jake.

'Come sit up by us,' she urged, and by the time they were both buckled up the jet was descending to land.

The villa was breath-taking Ellie thought when, two short hours later, the four-wheel drive Luca had hired finally came to a stop. They had driven through lush mountains, where both she and Jake had exclaimed at the glimpses they'd caught of turquoise strips of ocean in the distance.

Far behind them lay the buzz of the nearest town, replaced by hillsides dotted with whitewashed houses, and ribbons of tarmac winding away from the main road climbing the sides of the hills to disappear into the greenery.

All of it was barely visible because night had descended, although the villa itself was brightly lit.

It was peaceful, it was tranquil and it was telescopic-lens-proof.

'CCTV,' Luca pointed out as they headed to the front door. 'And the perimeter walls are crawling with cameras.'

'Extreme for somewhere you don't visit very often,' Ellie returned as she was offered a glimpse of how the really rich conducted their lives.

'I like my privacy.'

Which made Ellie think how furious he must be that it had been so efficiently invaded by his ex.

To Ellie, it had seemed like overkill. It was only after the first couple of days that she thought just how *safe* the place felt.

No prying eyes, and that lack of any intrusion from the outside world was like a pick-me-up tonic.

She had got through to her dad on the first evening they'd arrived and had stammered through an explanation for whatever tacky article he had read which, thanks to Lily, who was now back in the UK, had been all of them.

Then she had spoken to Lily who had been barely able to contain her curiosity and had asked so many questions about Luca that Ellie's head had been aching by the time she'd hung up.

But she hadn't been able to hold on to her worries for long because the villa was magical. Pale colours, shutters everywhere and a veranda that circled the entire house like a bracelet and was strewn with sitting areas. The breezes wafted through the open windows like a lullaby. The infinity pool was stupidly stunning, like something lifted straight out of a classy house magazine.

All the tension drained out of her body and, whatever charm the place wielded, Jake wasn't immune to it either.

His thin, pale face relaxed and the tentative advances he had shown towards Luca continued, slowly but surely. He began to play without reserve and to show some of the spirit a normal six-year-old boy should have.

On day one, they took it easy. Luca showed them around the villa. They strolled down to the private cove where Ellie sat in the shade reading while Luca spent an hour with Jake in the shallow water before calling it a day and retiring to take a series of business calls.

From where she was sitting, Ellie was able to hear their conversation, with Jake asking what fish lived in the sea, squealing apprehensively when the water got too frisky around his ankles and then finally drifting back towards her so that he could sit and focus on building a sand castle.

It was relaxed in the villa because Juanita, the house-keeper, was there, popping up with furniture polish and dust cloths in a very reassuring fashion.

She came in once a week, Luca told Ellie, regardless of whether the property was in use or not, to air it and make sure the roof hadn't fallen in. While they were there, she would come daily and also be responsible for all the cooking.

'So if you don't use this villa,' she asked, bemused by this display of wealth, 'then who does?'

'Friends.' He'd shrugged. 'Employees. Clients occasionally.'

'It's so beautiful. What a waste for you.'

'It's an investment. What's wrong with that?'

Ellie thought it was sad that he really couldn't see where the flaw in that argument was but she wasn't going to go down any more personal roads with him.

She was relieved when, on the first night, Juanita was bustling in the kitchen while they ate the dinner she had prepared after Jake had been settled. Luca had spoke to Juanita in fluent Spanish and then, meal over, Ellie excused herself and retired to bed.

Bit by bit, Ellie noted that the periods of time Luca spent with Jake increased. It was very small steps but all heading in the right direction.

She took a back seat, explaining to Luca that it was a good idea for him to have one-to-one time with Jake without her being there twenty-four-seven because when she was there Jake's attention was conflicted.

'Right now,' she confided when, on their third day, Luca and Jake had spent close to an hour together without Luca climbing the walls with boredom and looking at his watch, 'you're really making strides. Keep this up and by the time we get back to London, you can really begin the search for another nanny. Jake will be comfortable enough around you to see you as the primary adult in his life with the nanny as a secondary figure. He'll feel he belongs and that'll be more than half the battle won.'

They were on the sprawling veranda, Ellie sitting in a wicker chair with her book on her lap while Luca leaned against the wooden railing, looking down at her from his towering height.

Inside, Juanita, who had taken an instant liking to Jake, was continuing with her project to teach him Spanish. After all, as his godfather's heir, he would need to speak the language like a native.

Ellie stared up at Luca, shielding her eyes with her hand. Being alone had been rare so far. Juanita was around all the time, arriving at eight in the morning and leaving at seven, and when she wasn't around Jake filled the gap. Being alone with Luca was unexpected, and she had been lulled into complacency, so out here alone with him she was jumpy.

Just a handful of days in the sun had turned his skin to burnished gold, and there was a lot of that burnished gold on display, because he hung around in loose khaki shorts and tee shirts that did a brilliant job of showing off his lean, muscular physique.

Right now, his hands were jammed into the pockets of his cream shorts, dragging them down, which emphasised his lean hips and hard, washboard stomach.

She looked away quickly but her skin was prickling all over and she was suddenly self-conscious in her tidy pair of denim shorts and loose cotton tee shirt. And her bare feet. Somehow a pair of sandals went a long way to making her feel suitably attired.

'I hope,' she said into the lengthening silence, 'you don't feel that by giving the two of you time together I'm somehow shirking my duties...'

'If I felt that, trust me, I would tell you.' Luca raked his fingers through his hair. 'I can see that there has been an improvement in my relationship with Jake,' he admitted. 'So the last thing I would feel is that you're shirking your duties. You're doing exactly what I'm paying you to do. That said, you can relax in your spare time, Ellie. Have you been to the pool once since we got here?'

'I… Not yet…but I plan to…' She'd cringed at the thought of getting into her very proper, sporty black one-piece in front of him, choosing instead to watch from the sidelines while he and Jake took to the water.

'You can swim, can't you?'

'Yes! Of course I can swim! I was very sporty when I was a teenager!'

'Then enjoy the pool, Ellie. You can take the working hat off now and again.' He pushed himself away from the wooden railing and strolled towards her, then he leaned down, hands on either side of the chair, caging her in and bringing her out in a fine film of nervous perspiration.

'Luca…'

'You're beginning to make me feel like a taskmaster.' Luca watched the delicate sweep of colour in her cheeks and his keen eyes noted the way she had pressed herself so far back into the chair that she was in danger of breaking it. 'I'm not keeping tabs on you, Ellie.' His voice had sunk to a low murmur.

She smelled of flowers, fresh, clean and *young*. He found that he couldn't move because he was entranced by the delicacy of her face. She glowed over here. Her short hair had lightened in the sun and a sprinkling of freckles had appeared from nowhere on the bridge of her nose. She looked like a fairy. A ridiculously sexy fairy. He had to will himself to stand back, and when he did he made sure to put some distance between them, but his breathing remained thick and uneven.

'I know you're not,' she said evasively.

'Good. I'm going to work now and I'll be busy until early evening. Something has come up with a deal in Hong Kong and I have a series of conference calls to chair. Jake's busy with Juanita. You can sit out here reading your book or retire to your room, but you can also explore the grounds and enjoy yourself. If you like, I can arrange for you to be driven into the village. No one knows where we are so there's not much chance of any flash bulbs going off in your face. Besides, the village is small, and even if I don't get here very often I contribute quite substantially to various projects and organisations. They are reassuringly protective of my privacy.'

'I… I'm fine here, Luca. Thank you.' Her heart was thumping as though she'd run a marathon. 'I like reading, and I'm very relaxed, so please don't worry about me.'

For a few seconds he stared down at her, his expression veiled, then he straightened, eyes drifting downwards to the small, delicate points of her breasts. A surge of hot blood made his groin ache. He felt giddy, out of control, and he abruptly stepped back, scowling.

'Good.' His voice was cool and sharp. 'Just so long as you know that you can actually have fun—that you're not my servant, or on call twenty-four-seven.' At which, he swung away and headed at a pace towards his office.

Hurt by the abruptness of his voice, Ellie realised that whatever occasional shiver of camaraderie she sometimes felt with him, whatever weird feeling that he sometimes *saw her as a woman*, was an illusion because it was obvious the guy thought she was a bore. The sort who faded into the background and had to be forced to enjoy the massive grounds, the gardens and all the things that were on offer. She had brought her computer over and had mentioned that there was a backlog of school stuff to do, which had so far been put on the back burner. Hardly riveting stuff for a twenty-something singleton to be doing in a place the likes of which she would never, ever see again.

On the spur of the moment, Ellie headed straight up to her bedroom, slipped into her swimsuit, armed herself with sun lotion, a towel, a sarong and her oversized sunglasses and headed straight down to the cove.

Jake was with Juanita and, really, she'd had no time to herself since they had arrived.

It would be good to relax and enjoy the scenery without feeling self-conscious that Luca was around, or in teacher mode because Jake was there. What with all the business with her dad and his debts, relaxation had been a distant dream for so long now. She would be an idiot to pass up the opportunity to grab some while she was here in this little slice of paradise.

It was a little after five but the sun was still warm and the sound of the water whispering against the sand was soporific.

On the very verge of falling asleep, Ellie decided to take to the water. She'd represented her school in swimming and it felt great to be scything through the sea. It had been a long time. Public swimming pools were fine, but usually far too crowded to do anything but weave in and out of other swimmers, and there was nothing like the freedom of the open water.

Oblivious to everything but the feel of the water as she sliced through it, she was barely aware of the distance she was swimming.

After twenty minutes she stopped, lay on her back,

floated and let her thoughts drift in and out of her head. She closed her eyes.

Luca's sexy image swam into her head and she didn't bother trying to chase it out.

She shivered when she recalled how her skin had burned when he had touched her. She thought about the dark beauty of his face and the way his eyes lingered, watching her and thinking thoughts she couldn't begin to imagine but about which she could speculate for England.

She wondered...

Floating like driftwood, she wondered what it would feel like to have him touch her intimately. To have those long, clever fingers explore her body, rouse her passion. She could feel the warmth of her wetness mingle with the sea and she shifted, restless and suddenly aching between her legs.

She wanted to touch herself to ease the tingle there.

She wasn't expecting her lazy reverie and the pleasant ebb and flow of her fantasies to be brought to a sharp halt by the feel of someone grabbing her, gripping her waist and sending her into a panicked meltdown.

She thrashed like a wild thing as the sea water poured into her eyes and her mouth until she was spluttering and quite unaware, for a few terrified seconds, about what was happening.

Then she snapped out of it when Luca growled into her ear, 'What the hell do you think you're playing at!'

Her stinging eyes flew open and there he was, like a dark, avenging angel, glaring at her, out of his depth in the deep water but still holding her as though she was as light as a feather.

Ellie pushed, hands flattened against his rock-solid chest, and he circled her wrists with his fingers.

'What are *you* playing at? Let me go!'

'So you can bloody carry on drifting out to sea while you're in La-La Land? No way! You're coming right back to shore!'

'I'm fine!' Ellie yelled, dropping all pretence of professionalism, because she'd been taken by surprise, and because the feel of him so close to her, wearing next to nothing, was making her feel giddy and faint, especially when she'd been having such pleasurable and such, such taboo fantasies about him.

'You can't see the shore line, Ellie!' He was treading water but now he began to swim, making sure that she kept pace with him.

He was a strong swimmer, but so was she, and pride made her swim as strongly as she could so that he didn't think she was a wilting female in need of being saved from her own idiocy by a knight in shining armour.

By the time they finally made it to land, she was exhausted as she staggered upright.

He didn't wait for permission. Water pouring off him, he picked her up and ignored her half-hearted struggles against him.

'Put me down!'

'Shut up.'

'How *dare* you tell me to shut up?'

'Have you any idea how long you've been out here?'

'I must have forgotten my waterproof diving watch back in my room!'

'The sun's practically disappeared!' Luca roared, striding up the beach towards a rug that he had brought with him and dumped alongside her towel. 'You've been missing in action for over an hour and a half, Ellie!'

'No, I haven't!' The sun *had* begun to fade and… *An hour and a half?* Where on earth had the time gone?

In her raunchy thoughts! That was where!

She stopped struggling, choosing to hold herself as rigid as a plank of wood against him, which he ignored, and then she found herself on the rug, staring up at him and hastily shuffling herself into a half-sitting position, resting on her elbows.

She could barely catch her breath because the swim back had been so tiring.

Legs apart, Luca stared down at her, thin lipped, eyes narrowed, oozing anger through every pore.

'You suggested I take some time out,' Ellie said weakly. Okay, her eyes had been closed, and she might have dozed off out there, because darkness was rolling in at speed. Her heart was beating hard and fast.

'I didn't suggest you head out on a suicide mission into the open ocean! Do you know *anything* about the currents that can sweep along these shores without warning? Have you any idea how many people get into difficulties because they think that the sea is a safe place just because it's calm? No lifeguard here, Ellie!'

'Well, then.' She sprang to her feet, because lying on the rug just made her feel helpless with Luca towering over her like a skyscraper. 'Good job *you* came along to rescue me, isn't it?'

She was breathing brimstone and fire. This was a side to her that Luca had never seen. Her eyes were flashing, her hands were placed squarely on her hips and she was leaning into him with open aggression.

'Damn well is,' he growled. 'And there's no way you're going to attack me for being worried about your bloody welfare!'

'Well, I'm very grateful! Even though I *wasn't in any difficulty whatsoever*! How would you like me to thank you, Luca?'

'How? Well you can start with this…'

# CHAPTER SEVEN

HE KISSED HER. Even when he reached to cup his hand behind the nape of her neck and lowered his head Ellie still wasn't expecting him to *actually kiss her.*

The touch of his mouth against hers was as potent as an electric shock ripping through her body, heating her blood and firing her nervous system into frantic overdrive.

A soft kiss…but only for a second, just long enough to break down all her defences, and she stepped towards him, hands positioned to push him away but instead curving over his warm, naked skin and seeking out his flat, brown nipples.

She was straining up, on tiptoe, and she sighed into his mouth. She'd just been fantasising about this and it felt unreal for the fantasy suddenly to become bone-melting reality.

The teasing delicacy of Luca's kiss changed tempo and he pulled her towards him, tasting her with urgent hunger, tongues meshing, and their damp bodies sticking together, salty and hot.

Ellie's head fell back as he carried on kissing her and she wound her hands around his neck.

He was so impossibly strong and muscled and she

dropped her hands to trace the contours of his corded shoulders.

She was on fire, flames licking through her slender body, tightening her nipples and causing her legs to tremble unsteadily. As if sensing that, he swept her off her feet, without his mouth ever leaving hers, and this time when he rested her on the rug he lay down next to her.

Ellie moaned softly.

The sun was disappearing rapidly and they were bathed in soft twilight.

She squirmed against him, half of her aghast at what she was doing while the other half was sinking into the physical contact like a man deprived of water suddenly led to a flowing stream.

She'd never wanted anyone as badly as she wanted this man. She never wanted to come up for air, and she was so overwhelmed that 'right and wrong' and 'crazy and sensible' were just a jumble of words that made no sense.

Luca flattened her, hand on her hip, and he began stroking her thigh.

Her legs dropped open and he placed his hand over her crotch and gently massaged.

For a few seconds, she couldn't breathe. His touch was firm but he was caressing her in such a leisurely manner she could barely think straight.

She sifted her fingers through his dark, spiky hair and then felt the rough stubble on his chin and arched up to push her small breasts against his chest.

The damp swimsuit was an intolerable barrier, and when his hand drifted away from her crotch to cover her breast she hooked her finger under the strap, wordlessly leading him to do what she was desperate to do.

It was funny but *lust* was a word that had never exerted any curiosity for Ellie. She'd read a million articles about women who flung themselves into bed with some guy because he was irresistible.

Privately, that was a concept she had always held in contempt.

Really! Irresistible? No wonder the world was full of miserable divorced couples! If they were guided by lust, then where was the longevity in that? She'd always reckoned that her mum had married her dad because she'd been carried away by lust, only for reality to insert itself and begin its destructive work once the lust had tapered off.

She could never have imagined being swept off her feet and doing anything that went contrary to good, old-fashioned common sense.

She had watched and seen the way boys hung around Lily with their tongues out and their hormones all over the place. 'Recipe for disaster' was what she could have told them, and sure enoug, they always ended up retreating, wounded.

Even when she had had her one big affair with Paul, yes, Ellie had found him attractive enough, but she hadn't found herself wanting to fling herself at him.

In fact, the whole sexual side of things had been controlled and pleasant and that had suited Ellie fine.

She'd been devastated when he had succumbed to Lily's charms but not particularly surprised when, like all the others, he had fallen by the wayside as soon as her sister had decided it was time to move on.

Lust, Ellie had worked out a long time ago, was for the birds.

Except, caught in the grip of it now, she was finally discovering what all the fuss was about.

Luca's hands on her had the same effect as fire melting wax and her body was molten hot with need. She clung to him shamelessly and, when he eased the straps of her swimsuit down, she shuddered with heated anticipation.

It was dark now on the beach. The calm, glassy water was inky-black and the trees and rocks dark silhouettes against a starless horizon. The breeze was as ineffective when it came to refreshing their bodies as the whirring of a sluggish overhead fan.

But Ellie cooled as the swimsuit exposed the pert, rounded orbs of her breasts, pale in contrast to the rest of her, which had turned pale gold over the past few days in the sun. Against her pale breasts, her nipples were dark-pink circles, enticingly large compared to the size of her breasts.

Luca bent down, took one nipple into his mouth and began to suckle on it. He lathed the tight bud with his tongue and Ellie groaned and wriggled, feverish in her want.

Hand cradling the back of his dark head, eyes squeezed tight and mouth open as she breathed thickly, Ellie pressed him harder against her aching, sensitive breast, desperate for some attention to be paid to the other one.

She shuddered when he did just that, turning his attention to her swollen, pulsing nipple and, at the same time, easing his hand underneath the stretchy swimming costume to feel the slick wetness between her thighs.

'This is what heaven feels like,' Luca broke free to mutter. He meant it. She was so hot, so responsive and so damned sexy. It was as if he had discovered a different person behind the armour of prissy clothes—or had that person always been there? Had he seen the passion lying dormant behind the calm exterior? Surely he had, be-cause she had piqued his sexual interest long before now.

His erection was rock-hard and he had to control his breathing so that he didn't do the unthinkable. One touch from her and he knew that he would come as fast as a randy teenager, and he didn't want to do that. He wanted to take his time even though, at the back of his mind, he knew that they would have to stop. Right now, time was definitely not on their side.

But when?

Luca had no desire to lose the moment.

But the moment was lost when they both heard the distant reedy voice of Jake calling out for Ellie.

There was no way that either Jake or Juanita would take the steps that led down to the cove. They were lit but at this time of the evening it would be a hazardous trip down for a six-year-old and Juanita, despite living close to the sea, was terrified of water.

No matter.

That voice penetrated their cocoon and Ellie pushed Luca away with shaking hands and stumbled to her feet.

'What are you doing?' she cried, and it was such a stu-pid question that Luca didn't bother responding.

Ellie spun round and began running along the cove, grabbing her stuff en route, heading for the stone steps up to the villa.

Horror was spreading through her with toxic ferocity. How on earth had they ended up doing what they had? What had possessed her? How could she have lost all control like that?

*Lust*...was the word that sprang into her head, mock-ing and jeering at her prim, horrified reaction.

She recalled the feel of him in the water when he had

surprised her, the hardness of his body lying next to her and the sensation of his mouth on hers, on her lips…her breasts…her nipples.

She wanted to groan with frustration and despair because this sort of thing just *wasn't her.*

She headed up the steps at speed, half-stumbling as she neared the top to see Jake and Juanita on the lawn outside the front door.

Behind her, Luca was taking his time and not saying anything, and Ellie was more than happy to ignore him.

What sort of conversation could they have? The thought brought her out in a cold sweat.

She threw herself into scooping Jake up and hurrying inside. She knew she was chatting far too much, with high-pitched, feverish intensity, and she knew that it was to distract herself from the horror of remembering what had happened down there on the beach.

To her relief, Luca vanished, probably to bury himself in whatever he had been doing before he'd been rudely interrupted and taken it upon himself to play knight in shining armour.

It gave Ellie time to shower quickly, change and then return to the kitchen where she took up where she had left off with Jake.

'I was scared,' he confided in a small voice.

'And I was silly,' Ellie admitted, giving him a huge cuddle. 'I swam a little too far out, and that was incredibly naughty.'

'But Luca saved you,' Jake piped up in a voice that was full of admiration. 'When I told him I was scared, he told me there was no need to be because he'd make sure you were okay, and you were. He saved you.'

'I'm sure he'd like to think that.' Ellie couldn't help

injecting a touch of sarcasm into her response. 'Although I used to swim a lot when I was your age, right up until I was a big girl.' Which led to a long discussion about sports, hobbies and swimming and allowed her mind way too much freedom to roam and agonise over what she had done.

Ellie knew there was no way she could lay the blame on Luca's shoulders.

He had been dragged away from his work and had been furious at having to rescue her. Yes, he might have instigated that kiss, but she had flung herself wholeheartedly into it and had practically accosted the poor guy.

As if there was any chance that he could actually fancy her! Ellie cringed when she thought about that. He was a man and he had responded the way any man would have when a woman flung herself at him with abandon.

He had probably gone into hiding just in case she wanted a repeat performance.

Juanita had gone, Jake had been settled and Ellie was finishing the salad she had prepared for herself when she looked round to see that Luca had quietly entered the kitchen behind her.

She froze. She desperately wanted to blank him out but instead hungrily took in the lean, muscular lines of his body and remembered the way it had felt pressed up against her, wet, slick and hard.

'What are you doing here?' she questioned tightly.

He'd changed, as she had. Where she had got into some faded jeans and a tee shirt, he was in all black—a black V-necked tee shirt that clung in just the right way and black jeans. And he wasn't wearing any shoes. That seemed disproportionately intimate.

'It's my villa.'

'I... I've just eaten,' she gabbled, backing away as he strolled towards her then swerved to fetch a bottle of water from the fridge. 'I was just on my way up. I... I... I hope you remembered to say goodnight to Jake! It's a brilliant routine. Have I told you that? He really enjoys that.'

'We need to talk, Ellie.'

'Talk? Talk about what?'

'What do you think?' He raised his eyebrows and shot her a dry look.

He raised the bottle to his lips and began drinking and Ellie frantically asked herself how it was that someone drinking water from a bottle could look so sexy.

It was an effort to tear her eyes away and she had to work hard at channelling her thoughts into some kind of order.

So beautiful, she thought weakly. It wasn't fair! How was she supposed to stand a chance against someone so beautiful? She'd thought she was as tough as nails when it came to making judgement calls on men. She'd always found it easy to scoff at people who were swept away by something as superficial as *looks* because, after all, there was so much more to a person than appearances.

Yet here she was! Scratch the surface and what you found was a guy who had nothing at all in common with her, whose principles contravened everything she believed in, whose arrogance got up her nose...

It angered her so much that none of that seemed to count for anything because she took one look at him and something inside her melted. And then there had been those moments, like when she had seen him stooping down to Jake, slowing down, trying so hard to connect, willing to step out of his comfort zone. Those had been moments when something inside her had opened up, letting him in.

'I don't want to talk about that,' Ellie whispered.

'You want to pretend that none of it ever happened?'

'And none of it would have if you hadn't overreacted! I'm an extremely strong swimmer! I represented the county at one point when I was a teenager!'

'Academic.'

'What does *that* mean?'

'It means that whether you swam in the Olympics makes no difference to the fact that if we hadn't been interrupted we would have ended up making love on that beach.'

The colour drained from Ellie's face and then, just as quickly, rushed back to turn her cheeks beetroot-red.

'We wouldn't.' She turned away to busy herself by the sink. When she felt his hands on her shoulders, her whole body stiffened. For a few panicked seconds she forgot how to breathe. She didn't dare turn around to look at him.

'Why can't you just drop it?' she half-cried under her breath.

'And why do you find it so impossible to talk about it?'

'We would have come to our senses. *I* would have come to my senses. There's no way...'

'I wanted it, Ellie.'

'No! That's crazy!'

'And so did you.'

'Stop putting words into my mouth, Luca! Yes, I admit you're an attractive man, but that doesn't mean that I'm a complete fool!'

'Why don't you look at me when you say that? Or are you afraid to?'

'Afraid?' Ellie burst out laughing but even to her own ears her laughter sounded hollow. He'd thrown down a gauntlet and she turned slowly to look at him.

Luca dropped his hands and stood back.

'I apologise,' she said stiffly.

'For what?'

'For throwing myself at you.'

'I'm a big boy, Ellie. If I hadn't enjoyed it, I wouldn't have ended up lying on that rug with you, with the straps of that swimsuit down, feasting on your breasts.'

Ellie closed her eyes. Her breathing was laboured. She didn't understand why he had to be so provocative, so graphic.

'It was a moment of madness,' she whispered, help-less against the onslaught of wild emotion Luca's words had roused in her. Her body was responding in just the way she didn't want it to; she folded her arms protec-tively across her breasts and looked at him with deep reluctance.

'I want you,' Luca said flatly. 'I'm not saying it makes sense.' He raked his fingers through his hair, suddenly ill at ease but utterly unable to back away from what he wanted to say. 'I'm not saying that it's something I need. That either of us needs. But since when does everything have to make sense?' In his world, everything *always* made sense, and he was annoyed and frustrated that in this instance he couldn't bring his formidable intellect into play to control a situation that was, as she had said, no more than a moment of madness.

'I work for you, Luca.'

'And I have always kept very distinct lines between business and pleasure.'

He reached out to touch her cheek and felt her shiver under his touch. 'Until now.' He heard the unsteadiness in his voice with some surprise.

She was gazing at him, lips parted, pupils dilated, and she didn't pull away when he lowered his head and oh, so gently covered her mouth with his.

He tasted her.

This wasn't frantic and urgent, as it had been on the beach. This was slow and tender, and she lost herself in the moment, curving her body into his, her softness moulding against his hardness.

Their tongues were entwined and her eyes were closed as he took his time exploring her.

He wasn't rushing. He wasn't touching her anywhere at all and, the less he touched, the more she wanted him to. When he finally pulled back, they stared at one another in silence and he was the first to break it.

'I want to make love to you.'

'I don't understand why.'

'You do something to me. Have done for a while. There's something about you. I want to take you to my bedroom and I want to taste every inch of your body.'

'Luca…'

'Yes or no, Ellie? It's a simple question that needs a one-syllable reply.'

'I've never been the kind of girl who does this sort of thing. We're chalk and cheese…' She thought of the towering blonde mischief-maker who had been his last conquest. Men ran to type. Men who were attracted to towering blondes didn't suddenly find themselves unable to resist small brunettes.

But then again, small brunettes who went for serious, relationship-focused guys with a social conscience didn't suddenly find themselves unable to resist arrogant billionaires who expected the world to obey their commands.

So what was this about, for either of them? Was it because being here, in a place that was so peaceful and so magical, had turned their heads? Had it taken those first stirrings of attraction she had felt for him and magnified them into something irresistible? And was it all about novelty for him? A change being as good as a rest?

He was waiting for her answer. He said it was a simple yes or no but she knew it was far from that.

'Maybe opposites attract,' Luca murmured, because he couldn't think of any other explanation for why he found her so incredibly enticing. 'Yes, Ellie, or no? Say no and this is something that will never rear its head again.'

'Yes.' Apprehension and excitement flared inside her like a blowtorch. She looked at him and cleared her throat. 'Opposites attract. I guess that must be it.'

Luca wasn't sure whether to be flattered that she had agreed with him or disgruntled because it was hardly the level of adoring enthusiasm he was accustomed to from the opposite sex.

He wasn't going to waste time debating the issue.

'My bedroom?'

'This is so crazy...' But her head was so full of him that crazy made sense in a weird kind of way.

Wordlessly they headed for his bedroom. The effect of the silent villa felt like tacit encouragement, egging her on to do something that felt wildly, madly daring. She'd played it safe all her life and especially when it came to men. Living with a beauty queen for a sister, and a mother who wasn't backward when it came to drawing comparisons, Ellie had made a virtue out of never punching above her weight. Sensible choices meant she'd never be let down. Although that hadn't exactly worked with the boyfriend who had leapt for her sister faster than a Jack-in-the-Box, had it?

But still…

Heart racing, she paused as Luca pushed open the door to his bedroom and stepped inside.

Two banks of windows overlooked the sprawling back gardens and the windows were both open so that a cool breeze blew through, rustling the nude-coloured voile drapes. The bed was enormous. Ellie stood still and gazed at it. Was this really what she wanted—a meaningless one-night stand with a guy because she happened to find him irresistible?

Because she knew that, if it wasn't, then this was the time to back away.

'Cold feet?' He switched on the overhead light but then immediately dimmed it so that the room was infused with a mellow, warm glow. He turned to look at her, his beautiful face all shadows and angles.

'No,' she whispered, although she hadn't actually stepped into the room, but was hovering just outside, as though an invisible but impenetrable force field were keeping her out. 'You?'

'I don't get cold feet when it comes to sex.' Luca reached out and linked his fingers through hers, gently guided her into his bedroom and then shut the door behind them.

'Will you promise me one thing?'

'What's that?'

'We don't talk about this in the morning. I mean, we pretend it never happened.'

'We pretend it never happened...?' Luca murmured with low incredulity. Had any woman ever said that to him before? Nope.

'A one-off...' She placed her hands on his chest and stared at her pale fingers then raised her eyes to his. 'I've never done a one-off.'

'Nor have I.'

'Don't tell lies, Luca.' But she smiled and some of the tension left her. Of their own accord her hands were stroking his chest and loving the hardness of his torso under the tee shirt.

She was fascinated by the perfection of his physique. She itched to feel the flatness of his nipples again and to explore lower, to feel the throbbing pulse of him.

'I don't do one-night stands,' he murmured, cupping her rear and inching them both towards the bed. 'I may not do permanence but I don't do one-night stands.'

'So this is a first for both of us...'

'Both virgins when it comes to this, yes.'

Everything she said made sense and was what he should have wanted to hear. It was a complication that could end up a massive headache. She wasn't built like him. She still had ideals and illusions. She still believed in the power of love and all those fairy-tale stories that got people walking up an aisle before everything turned sour and the starry-eyed sweet nothings became high-pitched arguments in a divorce court.

She could get hurt.

'Just don't go falling for me.' He kissed the side of her face, trailed his mouth along her jawline, tasted the sweetness of her lips.

'That would never happen.' Ellie sighed and curved against him.

'That's good. We both know the score. This is an itch that needs to be scratched.' He nuzzled her neck and then broke apart to hook his fingers under his tee shirt, stripping it off in one easy movement.

He guided her hand to his erection, which was a prominent bulge under his jeans, and she gasped.

'My turn now,' he murmured into her ear, and he undid the button of her jeans and pulled down the zip, then worked his way into her panties until he found her sweet spot, the throbbing nub of her clitoris. 'Now touch me.' He groaned unsteadily as he slid his finger along and into her.

Ellie unzipped his trousers. She felt clumsy and gauche, and then nearly passed out when she actually touched him. He was huge, his shaft rigid and thick.

Touching one another without taking it any further was making her head swim. She was so wet between her thighs that she just couldn't keep still.

He broke from her but his eyes never left hers as he stripped off the rest of his clothes and then stood in unashamed glory in front of her. So lean, so beautiful, his physique perfect in every way. He let his hand rest loosely on his erection and smiled crookedly when she found she couldn't tear her eyes away from the sight.

'Your turn,' he commanded, watching.

Lack of experience showed in her first nervous fumblings, but when she looked at him the flare of desire was so apparent in his dark, intense gaze that her inhibitions were discarded along with her clothes.

She'd never thought of herself as desirable before and

that look in his eyes made her heady with feminine satisfaction.

It seemed hard to believe that this drop-dead gorgeous guy wanted her but he did. It was there in the flare of his nostrils and the burning darkness of his eyes.

In the grip of lust, Ellie was realising that there was so much more than love when it came to relationships.

There was...*this*. Wonderful, incredible, short-lived, like a firecracker burning bright until it was extinguished in a poof.

Somehow they made it to the bed. Her breathing was staccato-ragged.

He straddled her, and Ellie wriggled up to lick his thick, pulsing manhood, then he shifted and lowered himself to kiss her.

With a groan, she pulled him closer. He couldn't get close enough. She wanted to feel his body against hers, his heartbeat in tune with hers, his breathing warm against her skin.

Their lips met and she arched up to him, one hand behind his head, the other in a closed fist under the small of her back so that she was pressed against him.

Tongues meshed. Her groans merged with his. When he finally reared up, she wanted to do nothing more than yank him back again so that they could carry on kissing.

She had never dreamt that the physical demands of her body could be as powerful as this.

He pushed her gently on her shoulders and she tilted back, her small, pointy breasts a succulent feast waiting to be enjoyed.

She gasped as his mouth circled a breast, sucking deeply as his tongue teased the rigid peak. She couldn't contain her mounting excitement and she shifted her hips from side to side, and up and down, desperate and greedy for him in a way she would never have dreamt possible.

She was barely aware of panting his name or begging him to *hurry up because she couldn't take it any longer.*

She was breathing fast, and even faster when that devastating mouth finally left her breasts to trail a path down her flat stomach, pausing only to circle her belly button.

Luca parted her legs and with expert fingers stroked through her wet folds to tease her clitoris until her pants became hitched cries of pleasure.

Then he dipped down to taste her with the tip of his tongue, a gentle, delicate exploration that made her whole body stiffen in urgent response.

She curled her fingers into his dark hair, pressing him lower even as she opened her legs wider. She felt the waves of her climax begin to build, stiffening her body, and then, with explosive force, she spasmed against his questing mouth, bucking just as he'd said he wanted her to do.

She'd become a slave to her body. She'd reached heights that made her cry out in a voice she didn't recognise. She had no time to apologise for her premature climax, because surely it would have left him frustrated? She came down from her high and slowly he began to build her back up with expert finesse.

He knew just where to touch and how so that her sensitised body was once again roused.

When he sank into her, thrusting hard and deep, she was taken to whole new heights of pleasure, soaring and cresting, higher and higher as he plunged harder inside her, filling every ounce of her body.

Her climax this time was so powerful that it swept her away, and she cried out, jerking and arching as he angled his hips and his shaft in just the right way to take her soaring.

She felt him come, felt him stiffen on one final thrust, and then she was sated and so satisfied that what she wanted to do most was fall into a deep sleep.

Luca rolled off her, disposing of the condom she'd hardly noticed him donning, but then he immediately turned and pulled her close against him so that their naked bodies were pressed against one another.

'I should go,' Ellie said drowsily, although she didn't want to.

'I've decided to renege on my promise,' Luca responded without a hint of shame.

'What do you mean?'

'I still want you and I have no intention of waking up in the morning and pretending that nothing happened between us. A lot has happened between us, and one night isn't going to be enough for me. So, if you want to play the pretend game, then you're on your own.'

'But you promised!' Ellie said with consternation.

Luca shrugged. He circled his finger over a rosy nipple that was peeking out above the cover.

'Promises get broken. This one has.' He fastened his dark eyes on her. 'Are you going to tell me that one night will be enough for you? Because, if you do, then I'll say now that I won't believe a word of it. We're here and I don't intend to watch you from a distance and kid myself that I don't want to touch you.'

'We're not children, Luca! We're grown up enough to know that you don't always get what you want!'

'That's right. We're not children, we're adults, and we still want one another and we can have one another. Ten more days and then we return to London and this thing between us...this virus...gone. It's as easy as that...'

Luca was in no doubt that he would be more than ready to conclude things by then anyway. He bored easily and, though she might be stimulating now, in a fortnight that allure would have worn off, and it would certainly disappear under the weight of reality that would be waiting there for him. Besides, whatever ground rules had been agreed, he was still uneasy at the thought that she might start looking for more than was on the table.

'It's not as easy as that, Luca.' Her brain was refusing to function. It really wasn't as easy as that. Was it?

'Oh,' he murmured silkily, 'but it is. Trust me...'

# CHAPTER EIGHT

LUCA LOOKED ACROSS the width of the infinity pool to where Ellie was teaching Jake some swimming tricks of the trade. She swam like a fish. She could have rescued *him* if he'd been in trouble in deep water as efficiently as he had thought he'd been rescuing *her* a week ago when he'd spotted her on the distant horizon.

Now that he was looking at her, he decided that it beat reading the *Financial Times* on his tablet. She was so graceful, so slight, so supple when she moved, and she had a laugh that could light up a room. From behind his dark designer sunglasses, reclining on the lounger in the shade, Luca indulged in thinking about all the things he found strangely attractive about her, from the way she looked to the way she smelled and definitely the way she responded to him when he touched her. She was a firecracker between the sheets.

He was guessing that this was what a lot of people might call paradise. Overhead, the sky was a milky blue with just a few wispy clouds here and there to interrupt the perfect turquoise expanse.

The sun was beating down. At a little after five, it no longer bore the fiery intensity of the midday sun, but it

was still warm enough for them all to be out here fool-
ing around in the swimming pool.

Luca hadn't been to this particular property for some
time and the last time he *had* been, with a handful of
high-achieving employees being rewarded for their hard
work on a particularly fruitful deal, he had spent the majority of the long weekend working, signing off on yet
another deal, barely venturing outside except to a couple
of highly rated local restaurants. He hadn't been tempted
by the swimming pool and, indeed, he had barely spared
any time actually to appreciate his surroundings.

He was appreciating them now. Maybe it was because,
for the past week, he had seen them through Ellie's eyes,
and viewing his possessions through other people's eyes
was not something he spent a lot of time doing.

He had always been indifferent to the fact that women
found his wealth impressive. It came with the territory.

With Ellie it was…different. She was impressed, but
fundamentally she didn't attach a huge amount of importance to money, and she certainly didn't have pound signs
in her eyes at his displays of wealth. She teased him about
how much he owned and told him that he was too rich for
his own good. She was insistent that she do her bit around
the villa, always tidying up behind Jake, even though the
hired help descended every morning, paid to do that. He
didn't get it but he had to give her credit. She took absolutely nothing for granted and was at pains to explain
to him that, when you grew up with not very much, you
learned to appreciate everything you had.

When pressed, she admitted that, yes, some people
reacted by realising the importance of all those things

that money couldn't buy while others reacted by doing their utmost to get rich, whatever the cost.

Luca, in this roundabout manner, had found out about her sister and had formed a picture in his head of a woman who was very different from Ellie.

And of course, on rote, she reminded him how grateful she was for the way he had rescued her father.

'Which makes me think,' he had drawled as they had lain entwined in the sheets after a particularly energetic bout of love-making, 'that filthy lucre does, actually, have its uses.'

'Yes,' Ellie had said, 'it has purchase power. I can't deny that, but there's a lot more out there that can't be bought and, when you sell your soul for it, you lose sight of all those other things.'

'Very philosophical.' But Luca wasn't buying any of that because he'd seen too much avarice in his lifetime, and way too many women who would have sold their souls to the devils a thousand times over for money, but he was tickled pink at her sincerity.

'I have no idea how we got where we have.' She'd shaken her head in wonderment. 'Our perspectives on life are polar opposite.'

Luca didn't know, himself, how things had got to where they were between them.

The one-night-stand plan had been kicked to the kerb on night one, and their original intention to keep their liaison within the four walls of the bedroom had quite quickly got lost when he had absently held her hand in front of Jake.

Was that when, subtly, the relationship with his godson had changed? Had that been the turning point when Jake had begun to trust him? Yes, he had been making headway before, but things had definitely taken an up-turn at that point.

Luca guessed that this was as good as it got when it came to playing happy families.

It wasn't about love and it wasn't about selling your soul to someone else safe in the knowledge that sooner or later you were going to get hurt. Those were options he had shut the door on, and that was a door he would never thinking of opening, but yes...there was something to be said about this arrangement.

He gazed idly at his phone then re-read the text he had received from his PA, who knew how to handle the press with the dexterity of a magician, and whose contacts within those dubious circles had always been invaluable.

The salacious rumours started by his ex were about to go up a notch. It was becoming a headache. Being linked with a woman in a six-inch column in a tabloid was one thing. Taking the rumour that step further was something else.

Across the pool, Ellie was laughing at something Jake had said. She had a wonderful, engaging laugh, and for a few seconds, eyes concealed behind sunglasses, Luca watched her thoughtfully.

He thought that sometimes life had a funny way of dealing hands that looked unfortunate until you sat back and worked out how to play with them.

Under normal circumstances, he shouldn't have been here, but here he was.

If life had carried on as it had been, he would have been working and Jake would, in due course, probably have ended up in therapy because of him. Who knew? He might have suffered an even worse fate. Drugs...drink...

There was a world of temptation out there for kids who had been screwed over by life.

But this turnaround... Well, he couldn't have asked for better.

Luca stood up, glanced at his watch and strolled down to where the pair of them were recovering on the semi-circular marble steps in the warm, shallow end of the pool, exhausted after frolicking in the water.

Ellie shielded her eyes and watched as he approached.

Her heart flipped in her chest and her mouth went dry, her nipples pinched into tight buds, and every pore in her body responded in ways that were all too familiar now.

She didn't think she would ever tire of watching him, of listening to him, of the way he touched her, the way he made her body come alive.

For as long as was humanly possible, Ellie had kidded herself that the way he made her feel was down to lust. He was irresistible. She was too inexperienced to ward off the potent effect he had on her. She had capitulated and fallen into bed with him because her body had refused to listen to common sense, but the nature of lust was that it didn't last. She wouldn't be the first and she wouldn't be the last. Blah, blah, blah.

She didn't know when she wised up to the truth that what she felt for him—and it was a feeling that seemed to grow ever stronger by the second—left lust standing in the shade.

Unguarded, protected by all those common-sense check lists she had always had when it came to the opposite sex, or so she'd thought, she hadn't been prepared for her heart to be ambushed by the very sort of guy she should have been equipped to walk away from. She'd been side-swiped by his arrogance, his self-assurance, that way he had of always assuming that he was the leader and the duty of everyone else was to follow and obey.

She had barely really noticed when the little things had started piling up. The way he laughed. The occasional look of searing vulnerability she had seen when he looked at Jake, when he thought no one was observing him. His quick wit and the way he balanced his outrageous arrogance with magnificent generosity. He was a contradiction and he had sucked her in until it was hard to think of a time before him.

Where she had always imagined that love would be something that grew, after months of watering and nurturing, she had discovered, to her dismay, that it was something that just appeared from nowhere like a weed, with the power to smash her foundations to smithereens, and there was nothing she could do about it.

Except enjoy him while she could.

The end of their allotted time out was a heartbeat away and she intended to lose herself in loving him and then face the consequences when it was all over and she returned to normality.

She took great care in making sure he didn't suspect a thing, because she had her pride, and she couldn't bear the thought of him laughing at her, or looking at her with pity from the depths of those dark, fabulous eyes.

'Are you coming in?' she asked lightly now. She was already moist between her legs at the unconscious hunger in his gaze as he stared down at her.

She had brought her one and only black one-piece swimsuit, something she wore to the public swimming baths near her in London, because her other two were at the family house. It was so modest that she could have gone and done her weekly supermarket shop in it and no one would have batted an eye but, when Luca looked at her in it, it was as though she was the most stunning lingerie model on the planet.

Nothing could have made her feel more wonderful and more at home with herself and her body than that fierce gaze of unhidden approval and appreciation.

She'd discovered that it was like a drug and she knew that she was guilty of feeding off it, hungrily taking it in, because pretty soon it would no longer be available.

'Tempting,' Luca drawled. His dark eyes followed Jake who was splashing around with a toy Juanita had bought for him the day before. He turned his gaze to Ellie. 'Will you make it worth my while later if I do?'

Ellie blushed. 'Is sex all you ever think about?' she asked in a low voice as he settled on the stair next to her, leaning back and closing his eyes.

'No, work takes priority, but there's not a lot in it.'

'We should go in.' She stood up and called to Jake, then went to towel herself dry. Sex, sex, sex. It really was all Luca thought about. On every other level he was so complex and three-dimensional but, when it came to relationships, he was as shallow as a puddle.

'Just a minute, Ellie.' Luca held her arm, staying her, and when their eyes met his were so serious that she felt a shiver of panic ripple through her. 'Juanita's there. She can play with Jake for a couple of minutes, and I've arranged for her to babysit this evening.'

'Oh, okay.' His words were unthreatening but her panic levels were up all the same. 'I guess you want to discuss progress with Jake. I'm sorry. It's been far too easy to lose track of the fact that this isn't a joyride for me.'

'Stop.'

'Stop what?'

'Apologising for things you should never feel obliged to apologise for. We don't need to have formal discussions about Jake any more. We're lovers. Interviewing you across a desk is no longer relevant. I think we've gone past that point, don't you? But...there *are* other matters I need to talk to you about.'

'What other matters?'

'This isn't the right place. We need to talk and what I have to say will require a certain amount of privacy, hence the reason why I've arranged for Juanita to stay on. I'm going to book us into one of the local restaurants I recall as having excellent food, as well as a certain amount of privacy.'

Ellie felt the surge of tears prick the backs of her eyes because she knew what this talk was going to be about. She was about to get the 'Dear John' speech and icy fear settled in her heart. She looked away quickly but, when she next spoke, her voice was light, in keeping with the no-strings-attached, sex-only non-relationship they were supposed to be having.

'I know...' She shrugged and stared off into the distance. '"The time draweth near". We're going to have to wrap this up and actually start putting our heads together about finding a replacement for me. I've got a good idea of the sort of girl Jake would take to, and I don't think there's going to be any problems with adjustment.'

'Save the bracing words of encouragement, Ellie. Like I said, we need to talk, and a rushed conversation here isn't appropriate.' When he glanced down, he was treated to the sight of her cleavage, and the small bumps where her breasts were outlined by the fine fabric of her swimsuit.

He veered his eyes away from the delectable sight and breathed in deeply.

'I've got work to do. I wish I hadn't, but you're right. The time is drawing near and the rabble in London are getting tetchy.' He stood up. 'I'll swing by when Jake's in bed to tell him goodnight and then I'll meet you in the hallway.'

'Sure.' She followed suit, moving to fetch her towel from the lounger, along with all the other stuff that followed her out whenever she came to the pool. Sun cream, sunglasses, her sarong, her e-reader, her phone and an assortment of puzzle books she never got round to doing but always felt she might.

Luca veered off ahead of her to his office and she called out to Jake, but this time not even his six-year-old chatter could distract her.

It was the first restaurant they'd been to together since they had arrived at the villa and it felt odd to dress up when most of her time had been spent in shorts and tee shirts with flip-flops. She wondered whether his taste for shorts and tee shirts with flip-flops had reached the end of its natural cycle.

For the first time Ellie was nervous, and she wished that he could just text her the bad news, give her some advance warning so that she could get her facial muscles to behave and not let her down. Her stupid facial muscles were always letting her down when she was around him and she didn't want to give him any sign that there was anything amiss about calling it a day.

She'd brought a couple of summer dresses and, like

Cinderella stripped of the fancy ball gown, she looked at her reflection critically. Yes, she'd got a good colour out here in the sun, and, sure, her short hair was now streaked with auburn and gold, but aside from that... Now that she knew what this dinner was all about, now that her walking papers were about to be handed over, the ridiculous self-confidence he had inspired in her was seeping away like water down a plug hole. She was back to being who she really was. Just an ordinary woman whose moment in the spotlight was over.

Luca was waiting for her and she plastered a bright smile on her lips.

'I'm not late, am I?' She chatted as she slipped on the shoes she had carried from her room, dangling them on one finger. She didn't look at him but she was ultra-aware of him standing within touching distance of her.

He was coolly, elegantly sophisticated in a white linen shirt and a pair of dark jeans and loafers. The ultimate dream man, the stuff that women's fantasies were made of. She would have to work hard at making sure not to use him as a benchmark when it came to future relationships because, if she did, then she was going to be in for a rough ride.

'How was Jake when you went in to see him?' She settled on something impersonal as they headed out to the rugged four-wheel drive he had rented for the duration of their stay.

'Jake was...' Luca turned to her once they were in the car, before switching on the engine. 'Unrecognisable as the sullen little boy who first walked through the front door of my house seven months ago, but then you know how far I've come with him.' He smiled and slid his gaze across to her. 'Two days ago you gave me a gold star for progress.'

Ellie blushed when she remembered how he had demanded she reward him for that particular gold star. She also remembered telling him that he should aim for several a day because she quite liked the reward schedule he had in mind.

Bad time for that kind of memory. She decided to bring it down to business. It was what Luca understood best. Business and sex, and there was no way she was going to talk about sex. Or even remind him of what they had shared. She'd seen the way he had dealt with the ex who had ended up with her walking papers. She'd seen the annoyed impatience on his face because, once he'd dispatched a woman, the last thing he wanted was to have to go through the bother of working to disentangle her from clinging to his neck.

'Let's put the business chat on the back burner for the moment,' Luca drawled after she'd made a few fruitless attempts to discuss the qualities a replacement nanny might need. 'Talk to me about something else.'

'Like what?'

'Surprise me. I want some soothing conversation. I don't want to exercise my brain just yet with an in-depth discussion about what a successful nanny needs to be.'

'Well...what's the restaurant like? I... I hope I'm dressed okay. I haven't been abroad very much. Well, I can't tell you the last time, to be honest, but I always think that in hot countries the dress code is casual, even if the restaurant is fancy.' At this rate, Ellie thought desperately, she was going to exhaust her repertoire of nervous, pointless small talk before they made it to the restaurant.

For a few awkward minutes, Luca didn't respond, and

when he did it was to say, pensively, 'I had an interesting message from my PA.'

'Yes...?' Ellie shot him a confused look from under her lashes.

'My expectations that gossip about our so-called relationship would die a convenient death over the two weeks we were here seem to have been misplaced.'

'I don't understand what you're saying.' Ellie frowned because, in truth, she'd barely given a second thought to the silly rumours that had hastened their departure from London. She'd spoken to her dad when she'd first arrived. Her sister had been frantic with curiosity and Ellie had taken to dodging the calls and ignoring the text messages.

She was living in a bubble and there was no way she was going to let Lily burst it.

'My feeling is that Heidi had hoped for a more dramatic response from me when she spoke to the press. Anger, retaliation, a dialogue. Anything but silence. So she decided that leaving well alone wasn't going to do.' He looked at her and grimaced. 'There's nothing more dangerous than a woman scorned.' His voice had cooled. 'Especially one who clearly had a great deal more ambition when it came to our relationship than I ever had. Or, for that matter, ever hinted at. But we can talk about that over dinner.'

They'd arrived at the charming restaurant, white-fronted and cluttered with clambering, colourful flowers. The courtyard at the front was half-filled with high-end cars and she could see diners inside, outlined in mellow lighting. Inside, there were sofas, rustic wooden tables, little honeycomb-shaped private areas and so many plants that the oxygen levels must have been through the roof.

However, Ellie was too tense by this point to take it all in.

'What's going on?' she asked urgently, as soon as drinks orders were taken, menus inspected and decisions made about food.

'Hear me out without interruption.' Luca leaned towards her, elbows on the table, his lean, beautiful face unsmiling. 'The rumour about us has gathered pace and, on hearsay alone, the paparazzi will be printing a piece about our secret engagement. My PA has only managed to unearth this gem because she has some contacts with the tabloid press—a consequence, I'm afraid, of working for me. Naturally, she has neither denied nor confirmed the rumour. She thought it best to get in touch with me immediately.'

'Engagement? Secret?' Ellie blanched.

'The last thing I intended to do was to give credence to my ex's ridiculous rumours, because there would be nothing that would please her more than to think that she'd managed to throw my life out of joint.'

'You should have denied all that rubbish from the start!'

'I don't do conversations with hacks.'

'This isn't just about you, Luca!'

'There's no point crying over spilt milk.'

'Well, you're going to have to say something now. You're going to have to tell them that they've got it all wrong.' She thought about her friends who had been texting, and Lily who hadn't *stopped* texting.

'And naturally I will.' Luca sat back, sipped some wine and gazed thoughtfully at her over the rim of his glass. 'Although...'

'There's no *although* about it, Luca!' Ellie exclaimed

in dismay. Running through her head were the horrible and embarrassing ramifications of an article printed about an engagement that didn't exist. Luca might be able to ignore the gossip, because he didn't care what anyone thought about him, but *she* wouldn't. She would have to be the one to face inquisitive reporters and tell them that it was all a load of nonsense. She'd managed to laugh off the original article as malicious nonsense, and no one had questioned it because they all knew her, knew the sort of person she was. But *an engagement*?

'This is awful.'

'It's true that it's an unexpected development and yet… it's made me think.'

'Think about *what*?'

'Strangely enough, marriage. Not something I've wasted much time on.' He swirled his glass of wine, swallowed some and looked at her thoughtfully. 'My father never loved anyone but my mother and, when she died, so did he—or so did the better part of him, but you know that. However, he was a rich widower, and there was no shortage of gold-diggers trying their luck. They would have sold their mothers for a slice of his fortune. From every angle, love and marriage have never come out tops when put under the microscope. But…'

'But?'

'But although I don't do love…' he absently reached for her hand and played with her slender fingers '…and hence never considered marriage because the two seem to go together, I'm beginning to think that there can be another aspect to a very successful union. The situation in which we now find ourselves has opened up that possibility to me.'

'I have no idea what you're talking about. I *know* you don't do love so *what* situation and *what* possibility?'

'The second you entered Jake's life, things began to change. It was almost as though fate had decided that the wheels had to start going in a different direction. He met you and he immediately responded to you and you've brought out a side to him that I don't think anyone else would have been able to.'

'Thank you very much.' *She* did love, and it was just her bad luck and rubbish judgement call that had landed her where she was. Loving a guy who *didn't do love.*

'And things have only got better since we've been over here. I've talked more to him than I have done in the six months before and, if you don't think that we have extensive conversations now, then you're getting the picture when it comes to how little communication there was between us before.'

She opened her mouth to say something and he raised one hand to stop her.

'Hear me out, Ellie. Someone coming in to replace you isn't going to work in the way I originally thought it might. What Jake has with us, what this little holiday has made me see, is that we're family for him. The two of us. Not exactly the traditional family but one that seems to be working for him.' He raised his eyebrows. 'When it comes to traditional families, who's to say that they're any better than the non-traditional ones? So now it seems that, in the absence of denial, we're engaged. And why not?'

'I beg your pardon?'

'If the world thinks we're engaged, then who are we to tell them they're mistaken?'

'But we're not engaged.'

'Every word I say will probably jar with you, but I'm proposing that we continue our relationship, because it works, and not just for us, but for Jake.'

*'Continue our relationship?'*

'I'm asking you to marry me. For me, it's something that makes sense, and what I bring to the table would be considerable.'

Ellie's mouth dropped open. She wondered whether she had misheard him or maybe misinterpreted what he had just said. Or maybe that snazzy little fish starter she'd just eaten had contained some hallucinogens.

'You would never want for anything in your life again. You would have security and stability, and let's not forget the sex.'

'You're asking me to *marry you*? Because Jake's happy and because you and I rub along okay and have a good time between the sheets?'

'Doubtless, it's not exactly the romantic dream you've been harbouring…'

'No, it's definitely not that.'

She had a load more to say on the subject but she was side-swiped by the thought of her parents' marriage. That had started out as the romantic dream. It had descended into bitterness and resentment when the romantic dream had turned sour and her mother had realised that the middle manager she had married was never going to become anything more than a middle manager. A good man who would have done anything for her but who wasn't enough. She thought of her own upbringing. The way she had been casually side-lined by her vain and shallow mother, the way the relationship with her sister had suffered for that. She had had the traditional upbringing but it certainly hadn't been an entirely positive one.

'It's a crazy idea!' She robustly pushed that interrupting thought aside.

'Why? Because I'm not your ideal man?'

'And I'm not *your* ideal woman! You're in a different place to me, Luca. You see marriage as a business proposition with plus and minus columns that should all tally up to determine whether it's successful or not.'

She thought of Jake. Okay, so maybe he'd been lulled into a false sense of security, and okay, yes, maybe she and Luca had been remiss in being openly demonstrative in front of him, but she wasn't going to be steamrollered by Luca into thinking that the natural outcome of that was a walk up the aisle because Jake was in need of a family unit.

She could feel a tension headache coming on.

'There's no such thing as an ideal soul-mate, Ellie. We could make this work.'

'You don't love me.' *But could he learn to?* That possibility crept into her head like a thief in the night, and she shivered. 'And what happens when someone comes along to capture your interest? One of those women you've always been attracted to? Where would that leave this so-called business arrangement?'

'We could let this rumour stand and see how it plays out.' He sat back and watched her with a keen gaze. 'But when it comes to someone else coming along? You turn me on and I like you. Why would I want to look anywhere else?'

Ellie could think of a hundred reasons, starting and finishing with six-foot blondes with long, tanned limbs and big hair. He could talk the talk here, where there was no temptation, but what about when temptation *did* appear? What then?

'Don't dig deep to find faults with my idea,' he counselled levelly. 'Let's finish dinner, talk about anything but relationships and you can sleep on it.' He lowered his midnight-dark eyes then raised them slowly to look at her with frank appraisal. 'You can tell me what you really think when you're warm and drowsy after we've made love.'

# CHAPTER NINE

WITH THE DEXTERITY of a magician, Luca had spared no effort in pulling out all the stops to persuade her to his way of thinking.

He knew that she had her theories about soul-mates and the flowery promises of romance. He knew that his sensible suggestion for a union based on practicality was not high up there on her wish list... But there was this amazing chemistry between them and, however much she might waffle on about the importance of love, he knew that she had been sucker-punched by the power of their mutual physical attraction. She hadn't seen it coming.

She had never thought to work *that* into her long-term happy-ever-after plans.

And then there was Jake. He had watched them together and had seen the affection in her eyes when she looked at the boy. Would she be able to walk away from her little charge with the suspicion that she might take with her all the good work she had achieved?

From the heights of his cynicism, Luca knew that what he wanted was selfish. She was the glue between him and Jake. How successful would the happy family scenario be if a critical component of it went missing in action? He'd come far, but had he come far enough?

That aside, she was also a woman who appealed to him on many levels. The sex was stupendous but he could also appreciate her easy wit and the way she never deferred to him. Without the hindrance of wanting more than was possible, it would be a match that stood a better chance of working than any rush down the aisle between two starry-eyed people.

With the sharply honed instincts of a born predator, a man who always got what he wanted, Luca knew that making love was the way to get to her. He saw no down sides to using that ploy because to him it made perfect sense and bolstered his argument.

What he was proposing transcended the coldness of logic because it was infused with the passion of lust.

His fingers were linked through hers and he urged her up the stairs, stopping on every other stair to touch her. Action always spoke louder than words and he planned to put a lot of his persuasive powers into action.

Once in the bedroom, he kicked the door shut with the heel of his foot and propelled her towards his bed, stripping her off as they made progress across the floor until she was practically naked, with the dress pulled down and dropping to the floor as she shuffled backwards.

'Luca…' Did he think she couldn't see through his ploy?

'Shh…' He placed a finger over her mouth and then replaced the finger with his lips, kissing her without letting her surface for air.

He was doing what he did best. Pesky conversations could always be put to rest between the sheets, but this was bigger than a pesky conversation.

Ellie knew that there was still a lot more to say, but

when he was touching her like this, kissing her sense-less, rubbing his hands over her breasts, skimming them across her stomach, touching her between her legs…she lost the ability to think and turned into a mindless rag doll.

She fell back onto the mattress, arms spread wide, and watched with the usual level of shameless fascination as he stripped off in a hurry.

She could spend a lifetime doing this, she thought ab-stractedly, if she married him. They could give Jake the sort of stable home he would thrive in. *If* she married him. She'd be able to touch him whenever she wanted. *If* she married him.

But…but…but…

The agonising battery of questions tried to press onto her consciousness, but she didn't want to think of any of that, so she pushed them away and concentrated on the luxury of watching him stand for a few taut moments in front of her at the side of the bed, naked and unasham-edly aroused.

She propped herself up, then knelt and took him into her mouth. He had been a masterful tutor and she an en-thusiastic pupil, and she put all his lessons to use now as she licked and sucked him, feeling the rough ridges of his shaft, knowing just how to tease him until he was on the verge of losing control.

He juddered and urgently tugged her away from him, but then held her still for a few seconds while he re-grouped his self-control.

The sex was fast and furious, a tangling of bodies as they met their needs, pleasuring one another in ways that were so finely tuned that neither could put a finger on why, really, they seemed physically to meet with such ease and freedom.

Afterwards, spent, they lay back and eventually Luca turned to her, propping himself up on his side. He pulled down the sheet which she had hoiked up to cover herself because, to his amusement, she was always strangely prudish in the wake of their love-making; he traced a line over her collarbone with his finger.

'I won't lie to you, *querida*, my proposal is something that works for me. I don't do love and empty promises, but you add something to my life, and you add something to Jake's. Like I said, I never gave house room to thoughts of marriage, but this is an arrangement that has an excellent chance of success. It would certainly put paid to the nuisance of having to return to London and start pouring water on all the engagement rumour fires stoked up by my vindictive ex.'

Ellie knew that this level of honesty was commendable. He wasn't wrapping things up with pretty paper and ribbons and trying to pretend that what was in the box was more than it actually was. He was being truthful when he said that rumours of a phoney engagement had made him consider the advantages of a union that was actually for real. Jake would have a family. Luca would not have the bother of explaining himself to nosy reporters. As a bonus, he would have the satisfaction of knowing that whatever his ex had hoped to gain by stirring false rumours would be scuppered. And if he changed his mind? Well, it wasn't as though there was a wedding ring on her finger, was it?

'It all sounds very selfish, Luca.'

'Jake wouldn't agree.'

'So Jake wins and you win...and what about me?'

'You really think that love is a guarantee of happiness?'

'That's not the point, is it?'

'Well, Ellie, I think it is. We go into this with our eyes wide open. We respect one another. We get along. You'll have financial security for the rest of your life but, if you want to continue working, then that would be fine by me. I'm not a dinosaur who expects his woman to stay at home. Added bonus…the sex is great.'

'And what about when the sex isn't great any longer? Your track record doesn't exactly promise longevity on that front, does it?'

'You've broken the track record already. I'm not even beginning to be bored by you.'

'Because we've known one another for five minutes!'

Luca looked at her seriously. 'I've spent more undiluted time with you than I've ever spent with any woman in my entire life.'

Ellie hated the way hope had taken root and was making inroads. Hope that that meant something. Hope that he could come to love her. Hope that she could become indispensable. Things like that happened, didn't they?

'No girl dreams of a marriage proposal in the form of a business deal.'

'I don't get into bed with anyone I've ever done business with.'

'You know what I mean.'

'I can't force your hand, Ellie.'

'So if I say no, you wouldn't care one way or another?'

'I've found that life goes on, whatever disappointments crop up along the way. There's not much I've ever found I can't handle.'

'Because you've had to handle quite a lot from a young age…'

'Playing the therapist on me?' He wasn't nettled because he was enjoying looking at her. She was here, in his bed, flushed from love-making. This wasn't a woman who was going to turn him down flat.

'You're asking me to get engaged to you, and yet we don't even know one another.'

Luca burst out laughing, then manoeuvred himself so that she was resting in the crook of his arm. He played with her breast and brushed her hair with his lips.

'I think you'd be surprised at how much we know one another.'

'I'm not talking about sex.'

'Good,' Luca purred, stirring back into heavy arousal at the sight of her pink, pouting nipple. 'Because right now, there's too much talking going on. I'm happy to talk, Ellie, but only if the conversation is of the dirty variety. And don't tell me you don't want it. You know it turns you on when I tell you just what I want to do to your body...'

She opened her mouth and he shifted so that he was straddling her. He lightly ruffled the soft down between her legs and, while her body was busying itself trying not to succumb to what he was doing, he lowered himself, edging down to lick gently between her legs.

He teased the swollen bud of her clitoris until she was shifting with urgent little mewls of pleasure. He pressed his finger into her until she squirmed. He parted her thighs and hoisted her so that her legs were wrapped around him, allowing him to explore her wetness without hindrance.

He touched her everywhere until there were no more words and no more questions.

If she had doubts about his proposal, then this was as effective a way of showing her what, exactly, would be on the table.

Ellie wondered whether the proposal and her ambivalent response would affect their relationship but the following morning nothing was mentioned and there was no coolness from him.

Had he forgotten about it or just shrugged off her negative response as *'one of those things, you win some you lose some'*?

She didn't bring it up and nor did he. Luca wasn't accustomed to obstacles and either he had decided to jettison the idea because he'd hit a bump in the road, or else he was playing a waiting game.

Either way, Ellie wasn't going to be put on the back foot by bringing it up.

Nerves all over the place, she could barely focus on the day trip to a secluded bay that Luca took them on on a small motor boat he kept. It was a billionaire's plaything that was small, compact and kitted out to an eye wateringly high standard. The fabulous picnic which had been prepared for them tasted like cardboard to Ellie. She swam and did a little nature tour with Jake, and she knew that she said all the right things and held his interest for the full forty-five minutes as they walked and looked at stones, plants and rock pools, but she was so keenly aware of Luca, there right alongside her. So sexy, so tempting…so *suddenly attainable*…

It was a relief when seven o'clock rolled round and Jake was settled in bed. For the first time, when Ellie asked whether he wanted Luca to read him a story, he shrugged and said, 'Okay, I guess so.'

Major headway. Prompted by the security of the family unit he thought he now had...?

Luca was waiting in the kitchen when she entered at a little after seven-thirty, his back to her as he stared out of the window. But, before she could say a word, she felt the buzz of her mobile phone in her jeans pocket and she absentmindedly pulled it out as she headed into the kitchen, moving towards Luca.

'Lily!' For a few seconds, Ellie was so disorientated that she couldn't quite match the sound of the voice on the end of her phone to the sister whose nosy text messages she had been studiously ignoring. 'Is Dad okay?' A feeling of nausea crept into the pit of her stomach. She'd been living in a bubble. The sound of Lily's voice was the pin that had been stuck into that bubble, bursting it immediately. It was the harsh sound of reality and it made Ellie feel suddenly sick.

'You haven't been answering any of my texts!'

'Sorry, Lily. I'm back in a few days and I thought I'd... er...wait and, you know, talk to you face to face.'

'I've looked this guy up online and he's loaded, Ellie! Plus he looks like a rock star. So what the hell is he doing getting engaged to you?'

'Thanks very much!' Ellie bit down the temptation to press the disconnect button on her phone. She knew her sister so well. Lily wasn't about to congratulate her on landing a great catch. Lily was thinking ahead, working out how much more suitable a guy like Luca would be for *her*...

'You know what I mean. Remember boring Paul Jenna?'

'I try not to, Lily,' Ellie said through gritted teeth.

'Dad says you told him that it's just a load of nonsense. Is it?'

'Let's not talk about me.' She glanced at Luca who was shamelessly earwigging into the conversation and staring at her with undisguised interest. 'Let's talk about you.' Usually this was guaranteed to get Lily off the thorny subject of Luca. 'Tell me what you've been up to in America. Lots of important…er…exciting jobs and offers?'

'Have you slept with him?'

'Lily!'

'Okay. Out of order. Sorry.'

'How are you enjoying being back in the UK?'

'Finally! She's asked the question! I'm not in the UK! I'm calling from your part of the world! Dad told me where you were and I thought I'd fly over and pay you a visit! He's worried.' Lily's voice was suddenly pious. 'So I offered to check and make sure you're okay.'

'You're…*here*?' Ellie looked around her wildly as though anticipating a dramatic entrance from her sister via a cupboard.

'Just making sure you're not in a pickle! You have to admit it's not every day you get engaged! I know what Dad said, that it's all a load of rubbish, but still…what are sisters for if not to look out for one another? Anyway, Els, I'm running out of juice on my cell phone, so text me the address, would you? I'll take a taxi.'

Put in a position from which there seemed to be no easy way out, Ellie gave Lily the address. Her head was swimming, though. How long would it take her sister to hit the villa? How long did she intend to stay? As expected, there was no shame on Lily's part when it came to showing up uninvited at a stranger's house.

*Because there would be an agenda.*

*If, once upon a time, her sister had nabbed the guy
Ellie had been seeing just for the hell of it, then what
might her intentions be when it came to a man like Luca,
the most eligible man on the planet?*

Only now did Ellie realise that she had actually begun
to give house room to Luca's crazy proposal. She might
have laughed at his preposterous marriage proposal but
it had set up a series of tantalising scenarios. Lily showing up on the doorstep? It didn't bear thinking about.

Five minutes later, Ellie was staring at the phone and
feeling as though she'd been run over by an HGV.

'Family?' Luca encouraged.

'My sister.' She heard a note of dismay creep into her
voice and she summoned up a smile from somewhere.
'Guess what? She's here, right here, a taxi ride away,
and she's coming to visit. I can't wait to see her. It's been
months and months…'

'Ah, the famous sister you think is right up my alley.'

Ellie stiffened and remained silent. He extended a
glass of wine to her and she swallowed it in one gulp.

'Dutch courage?' he murmured with keen interest,
and Ellie blushed.

'Thirsty.'

'For wine. Interesting. Normally a glass of water does
the trick when it comes to quenching thirst. You should
sit down. You're looking a little green round the gills.'

'I should tell you that she knows about the…er…fact
that…well… I happened to tell Dad ages ago that if he
read some silly nonsense about us being together then
it was a complete lie and he wasn't to believe a word.'

'And now that there's an engagement story doing the
rounds and your sister thinks that there's no substance
to it…'

'Something like that.'

'And would she be right?'

Something wicked and daring nudged past the sudden onset of anxiety Lily's call had generated.

Wow. How dared her sister be so openly shocked that Ellie could actually be engaged to someone gorgeous, rich, exciting and *eligible*? How dared Lily take it as read that the engagement thing was obviously a sham?

And why should Ellie automatically begin surrendering at the thought of her sister coming along? Why should she just lie down and wave a white flag simply because she knew that Lily would get the guy, as she always did?

Ellie was suddenly sick of all the insecurities she always seemed to have to put to bed whenever Lily was around.

Luca had given her confidence she hadn't known she possessed—why should she dump it all because Lily was coming out here on a fact-finding operation? A so-called fact-finding mission because sisters had to look out for one another. Since when had Lily ever played by those rules?

For the first time in her life, Ellie had done the unthinkable and stopped playing it safe. And it felt good.

'We could take a chance.' She threw caution to the wind along with her long list of pros and cons.

Engagements didn't always lead to weddings… They *could* take a chance. So Luca didn't love her, but she could have some stolen time to try and make herself indispensable to him and, if that was through Jake, then so be it.

She couldn't bear the thought of never seeing him again and why kid herself that that was something she would be able to handle?

Luca smiled a slow, lazy, satisfied smile and drew her towards him. Then he kissed her and all the doubts she had had about this wild decision flew out of her head with a whoosh. She reached up to link her hands around his neck and kissed him back with hunger and abandon.

Was she doing the right thing? This felt like a little rebellion but it also felt good. She couldn't suffocate that little sliver of hope that what she and Luca had cultivated over the weeks would be strong enough to counter the Lily effect.

She was trembling as her slight body pressed against his rock-hard erection.

For some reason, that phone call had galvanised her into accepting his proposal and Luca wasn't going to question it.

'You're making the right decision,' he murmured, drawing back to look at her, while gently sifting his fingers through her short hair.

'You *would* say that.' Ellie's voice was breathless and teasing. 'If someone agrees with you, then you're always going to think that they're making the right decision.'

Luca grinned. 'But I'm always right,' he said piously, making her smile, relax and momentarily forget the fact that her sister was heading towards her at speed, a force to contend with.

'Stop looking so anxious,' he counselled, kissing her again and pulling her against him.

'My sister has always had that effect on me,' Ellie confessed, resting her head in the crook of his neck.

'Makes you anxious? Charming.'

'Charming,' Ellie muttered inaudibly, 'is exactly how you'll probably end up describing her.'

'Come again?'

'Nothing.' She smiled up at him and squashed the thread of apprehension running through her. 'Anyway.' She stepped back and tidied herself and decided that some more wine was necessary. 'She'll be here shortly…'

But it was another twenty-five minutes before the doorbell went. Ellie dashed out while Luca waited in the kitchen, intensely curious to see what the sea had decided to wash up.

He had a rough idea of what to expect and he wasn't disappointed.

'Luca, this is my sister, Lily.'

Ellie watched the interplay with eagle eyes and, to Luca's credit, if he was impressed then he wasn't showing it.

She felt an uncharitable spurt of satisfaction because Lily, just his type, was even more stunning after months spent in the Californian sunshine.

She had been toasted golden-brown and her long white-blonde hair fell in a glossy curtain down her back. She was dressed in next to nothing—a little crop top that rose to reveal her firm belly and the tattoo of a swallow just below her belly button, low-slung ripped jeans that seemed designed to show off legs that went on for ever, and flip-flops.

Plus she was in full flirtatious mode, talking quickly with lots of engaging hand gestures, and using her body language to suggest that what he could see was only the tip of the iceberg.

Ellie had seen her sister in action a thousand times but her heart was still thudding painfully because this was the first time she was really sickened at what might happen if she weaved her magic charm and sucked Luca in with those big, blue eyes.

'You'd take to life over there like a duck to water,'

she was trilling as she tossed her blonde mane over one shoulder and made herself at home at the kitchen table. 'It's full of movers and shakers in the media world and you'd really fit in. Have you ever thought about making a movie? I have a lot of connections…not that you'd need any!' She dimpled a smile, batted her lashes and pouted. 'I know you've gone out with a number of celebs.'

'Not my thing,' Luca responded politely.

'You could even be an actor.' Lily tilted her head to one side and looked at Luca narrowly while, standing to the side, Ellie gritted her teeth. 'You have just the sort of dashing, dark looks. Such a catch, Els!' She winked, making sure that Luca saw that wink, making sure he knew that she knew that it was all an act.

'I'm going to catch up on some work.' Luca was making for the door. 'Give you two time to catch up.'

Ellie hovered, but in the end didn't say anything, because she was too busy agonising over her thoughts. She'd just agreed to his proposal but was already beginning to see the holes in it. Here in Spain, in this bubble, it was easy to forget the outside world. Lily had wafted through the door, bringing that outside world in with her, and Ellie questioned whether, once they were back in London, Luca would be able to resist the charm offensive of all those beautiful Lily lookalikes who flocked around him. Playing happy families because of his godson might begin to look a little less alluring.

'He is *gorgeous.*'

Startled out of her introspection, Ellie moved to top up her sister's glass and asked politely, 'Have you eaten, Lily? I could fix you something.'

'Ever the home maker. No thanks. Dieting.' She patted her stomach. 'You wouldn't believe the competition out there.'

'But it's going well? You've barely mentioned what you've been up to.' *Too busy flirting with Luca.*

Lily brushed aside the show of interest and strolled through the kitchen, taking everything in. 'Course it's going well. Why wouldn't it be? Anyway, I would have helped out with Dad, you know that, but it was a bad time financially for me just then. You have to invest to create and just then I'd sunk quite a bit into portfolios and the like. You know how it is.'

Ellie had no idea.

'But, doesn't matter now anyway! Tell me all about the hunk. I know you're just here for the kid but you two must, you know, socialise now and again... Fill me in.'

Ellie began opening cupboards, fetching stuff from the fridge, ignoring her sister and the avid curiosity etched on her lovely face.

Lily hadn't come to make sure everything was okay. She had come because curiosity had got the better of her. How had the sister who had always faded into the background suddenly found herself in a position where she was being written about in a gossip column? Was there any truth behind that engagement story? Surely not?

'When was the last time you ate?' She knew that she was clinging to her composure by a thread, fighting against habits of a lifetime which compelled her to fade into the background.

Because she *had* accepted Luca's proposal, hadn't she? She really *was* going to have a ring on her finger, wasn't she?

Admittedly, it wasn't actually there yet, and would probably not materialise now that Luca had been given a tantalising glimpse of the sort of thing he'd been miss-ing out on ever since he had become a hermit living in a villa in the middle of nowhere, but still…

In a flash, Ellie knew that Lily would make a pass at Luca without a second's thought.

Just as she had done with Paul.

Lily would make a pass at Luca because he was the sort of man she had spent her entire adult life trying to get. He was rich, he was powerful, he was good-looking. He was the kind of man that other people hung around, looked up to and tried to be friends with.

He was, in short, the ultimate catch.

'I told you, Ellie, I'm not hungry. Stop fussing and sit and tell me about Luca. Is he single? I mean, really? Or is there some celeb stashed away somewhere waiting in the wings until this whole stupid engagement nonsense blows over?'

'Why do you ask?' Ellie's voice was tight as she sat in front of an unappetising omelette and dug into it, mak-ing sure not to look at Lily.

'Okay, tell me if you're all right with this—and I'm sure you will be—but if he isn't taken then I might, you know…'

'No, explain.'

'Well, he's pretty fabulous, and I'm not going out with anyone at the moment. So many gays out there, you wouldn't believe, and most of the guys I meet are a lot more into themselves than they are into me. None of them can walk past a mirror without crashing into it.'

'I'm sorry to hear that,' Ellie said with genuine sym-pathy because, like a plant needed nutrients, Lily needed the adoration of men to thrive.

This was the first chink in that coat of armour her self-confident sister always presented to the world.

Which didn't mean that Ellie was going to let herself fall right back into the status quo, fading into the background and accepting that her sister would always get what she wanted because of how she looked.

'Well.' She sighed and pushed her plate away from her. She linked her fingers on the table, then looked gravely yet kindly at her sister. 'I hate to be the bearer of bad tidings, Lily, but as matter of fact Luca is most definitely taken.'

'Is he?' Lily narrowed her eyes and Ellie could see her mentally working out how she could trump the opposition.

'He is. By me.'

'You're having a laugh, Els.'

'I'm not. The fact is…we're engaged. For real.' Empowered, she sat back and cocked her head to the side, as though deciding how much to tell and how much to withhold. Her heart was hammering inside her chest. Her skin was clammy at the enormous leap into the unknown she was taking. 'Okay, I admit when that story first broke about us seeing one another it was all a load of bunkum. Luca had taken me to a country pub to discuss Jake, and his ex had shown up and seen us together and then decided to wreak a little havoc.'

'I can't believe this.' Lily was flabbergasted. Ellie could have told her that the sky was falling in and she wouldn't have received a more stunned reaction.

'And then there was that business in the tabloids about an engagement. By then—and this is just between the two of us—Luca and I were…well…*you know*…'

'Sleeping together?'

'Falling in love. Truly, madly and deeply. I don't know how it happened, but I tell you what, it's the most wonderful thing I've ever felt in my life.' She could feel herself welling up. Lily might think she was welling up with tears of joy. Ellie knew that she was welling up because the picture she was painting was half-true and she wished that it was all true.

'He's terrific, Lily. He comes across as arrogant at first, but as soon as you get to know him you see that there's so much more to him than meets the eye. He's smart, funny, thoughtful, and incredibly frustrating sometimes, but I don't think I could love anyone as much as I love Luca.'

'And he feels the same way about you?'

'Why else would he have asked me to marry him?' Ellie neatly evaded a direct answer to that question.

'I don't see a ring on your finger.'

'That's because he wants to take me to his jeweller's in London when we get back. Don't forget, this wasn't planned. I mean, it's taken both of us by surprise. But, when love strikes, what can a person do?'

She laughed gaily, stood up to take her dishes to the sink, simultaneously avoiding her sister's sharp, probing eyes, and heard a deep, dark, velvety and very familiar drawl behind her.

'What indeed?'

Ellie swung round, almost dropping the plate and glass because her hands were suddenly as slippery as if they were coated in oil.

Her mouth fell open and colour rushed to her cheeks in a tidal wave of bright red.

'Luca!'

'My darling.' Luca looked at Lily whilst strolling

across to wrap his arms around Ellie, before dipping to kiss her on the side of her mouth. 'I'm very glad you listened to me and told your sister about us.'

He turned and pulled Ellie towards him so that he was standing with his back to the kitchen counter with Ellie in front, her back against his stomach, his hands draped loosely over her shoulders.

'She wanted to break it to her dad at the same time, put paid to all those pesky rumours doing the rounds. Yes, it may have been a piece of malice on the part of my ex coming up with that story, but how was she to know that the engagement she'd fabricated would turn out to be the real deal?'

Lily made a strangled sound and rose to her feet, suddenly looking very young and vulnerable in her confusion.

'So, just for the record,' Luca said without batting an eye, 'I'm not up for grabs.'

'I... Well, of course...'

'And I know you wouldn't be so tactless as to make a pass at the man your sister intends to marry, but if you do you should know that I wouldn't take to it kindly.'

'I wouldn't dream of... No... Well, congratulations to both of you. I'll... I'm off to sleep and I'll leave first thing in the morning!'

'I'll make sure there's a taxi waiting for you. You can have full use of my private jet. Say eight-thirty tomorrow morning?'

The silence that settled as Lily shut the door behind her could have been cut with a knife.

Luca slowly turned Ellie round to face him.

'Well, well, well...'

# CHAPTER TEN

ELLIE CATAPULTED HERSELF out of his arms and spun round to face him, arms folded defiantly, eyes blazing.

'How long have you been standing outside that kitchen door *eavesdropping*? Do you think that listening to other people's conversations is *acceptable*? Because *I don't*!'

'Totally unacceptable,' Luca conceded smoothly. 'But I couldn't resist once your sister started asking whether I was open territory. I was curious to see where the conversation was going to go.'

'Lily's always thought that she could do what she wanted when it came to guys,' Ellie gritted stiffly. 'I was just being *human* when I decided to show her that there were limits!'

Luca poured himself a long glass of water then pulled up a kitchen chair and sat down. 'Let's talk.'

'Let's not.'

'Forget about those declarations of love for a minute. I want to ask you about your sister.'

'Why?'

'Ellie, stop inching towards the door. We either talk here or we talk in the bedroom but we're going to talk.'

'Isn't that a bit dangerous, Luca?' Ellie threw back at him. She was frantically trying to work out what, exactly, she had said. Lots of incriminating stuff. She'd poured her heart out to Lily, blissfully unaware that the wretched man was lurking outside the door with a glass pressed against it, hearing every word.

'What do you mean?'

'*Talking.* Isn't *talking* dangerous for someone who likes keeping it superficial? For someone who gets into a panic if there's a woman in the kitchen with a frying pan in her hand and a recipe book on the counter? Isn't that why this *arrangement* of ours is so convenient for you, because it bypasses all that nasty domestic stuff you feel trapped by?'

'If we get married, then I'm assuming you'll have a frying pan in your hand and a recipe book on the counter from time to time. Did you think that your sister was my type because of the way she looked? And for God's sake, stop hovering! Sit down.'

'Stop yelling at me,' Ellie muttered, shifting to sit, mostly because her legs were beginning to feel wobbly.

He was tying her in knots. He didn't do love and he didn't do domestic. What he did was *business arrangement; no emotional ties, thanks very much.* So why wasn't he peeved at the thought of her doing something such as cooking for him? Wasn't he suspicious that that might be the start of something unfortunate?

She looked at him in defiant silence.

'Answer my question.'

'Of course I thought that! She's blonde and beautiful and she's not backward at coming forward!'

'I'm surprised you didn't give her the green light to strut her stuff for me,' Luca said drily, and Ellie reddened. 'It crossed your mind, didn't it?' He looked at her narrowly, his dark eyes cooling by several degrees, and she shook her head.

She felt drained. So what was she going to do now? How was she going to handle this situation? Lie? Pretend? She was fed up pretending.

If he was so keen for them to talk, then talk she would, and she was going to tell him the truth—how she felt, when she'd started feeling what she felt, what she really wanted out of any relationship with him.

If he didn't like it, then he would be free to walk away.

She'd been stupid to buy into the notion that marrying him was going to be the better option because she would be able to indulge her love for him and then maybe, just maybe, he might start returning some of that love.

This arrangement had been formulated with Jake in mind. If Luca had any feelings for her at all, then they largely revolved around feeling *turned on* because he fancied her, and that didn't count.

Okay, so maybe he liked her well enough, but that wasn't love, was it?

Was she really going to be satisfied with him *liking her well enough*?

Wouldn't it be better for her, in the long term, to walk away and hope that one day she might meet a guy who could love and cherish her the way she deserved to be loved and cherished?

Yes!

'No,' Ellie told him truthfully. 'It really didn't occur to me. Or if it did, I barely registered that. Thing is… I had a boyfriend once. His name was Paul and I thought that it was the real deal. That was a couple of years ago. He was a good, solid guy. Really nice. Very caring.'

'Sounds deadly.'

Ellie frowned and realised that Paul, whilst ticking quite a few boxes, hadn't been a riveting match, especially when she compared him to Luca.

'He wasn't at all Lily's type,' Ellie mused, gazing off into the distance. 'Lily always went for good-looking, solvent and hunky. But she turned her attention to Paul. I don't know if she did that to be mean, or if she did it unconsciously because flirting with guys just came as second nature to her. Anyway, whatever. He fell for her hook, line and sinker. One minute, he was talking about holidays and a life together with me. The next minute, he was drooling after my sister. So was I tempted to tell her to have a go with you, if that was what she wanted? No.'

'In fact, you decided to do just the opposite,' Luca murmured, expression veiled, and Ellie shrugged and looked away.

She now expected him gently but firmly to set her straight on what he had overheard. Probably tell her ruefully that there was no way he could fulfil the arrangement because he wasn't looking for what she wanted.

'I'm only human.'

'Has it always been like that?'

'Like what?'

'Living in your sister's shadow.'

'Pretty much. She had the looks and my mother cultivated that. She wanted Lily to succeed where she thought she had failed. My mother was a disappointed woman. She was very beautiful, and I think she thought that she deserved more in life than to be married to my dad, who was just an ordinary guy.'

'An unhappy marriage,' Luca murmured. 'And yet you still have all those romantic notions about love and marriage.'

'What's wrong with that? Because my parents didn't have a good marriage, doesn't mean that good marriages don't exist.'

'Did you get a kick out of telling your sister that the engagement was for real?'

Ellie blushed and said grudgingly, 'Huge.'

'Bigger question coming here. Did you mean any of it?'

Ellie looked at him. This was it. Crossroads time. She had a choice. The truth would free her, whatever the outcome, whether he fled the scene in terror or not. But a little white lie was so much more compelling...

She would be able to clear off with her pride intact and her head held high. She could laugh gaily and tell him that *of course, she hadn't meant a word of it!* He'd laid down the rules of the game and he would be relieved that she had stuck to them.

'All of it.' Her eyes were clear and steady, and she took a deep breath and forced herself not to look away. 'Every last word. I'm sorry. You warned me enough times about keeping emotions out of this, and I wish I could have done that, but I couldn't.'

Ellie wished he would say something. Anything, really. But he just sat there, very, very still, his dark eyes revealing nothing. Which meant that she had to play a guessing game, and she hated that.

However, now that she had started, she felt compelled to carry on and lay herself bare.

'I'm in love with you. I know you never signed up for that, and I know I probably shouldn't be telling you this because you're the guy who's locked his heart away somewhere and thrown away the key, but there you go. I'm in love with you. I don't know why or how or when

I fell in love with you. I wish I could be noble and say that I agreed to the whole engagement thing because I thought Jake would benefit from having both of us on the scene, and I suppose there was a bit of me that was persuaded by that argument, but truthfully? I wanted to do something out of the box just for once in my life and I also thought that, if we did end up together, I might stand a chance of somehow getting under your skin.'

'I have never let any woman get under my skin.'

Ellie cringed, even though he wasn't exactly saying anything she didn't already know.

'I know, but you've never been engaged to anyone before, have you?' she threw at him. 'Or have you?'

'Never been stupid enough.'

'Why are you so cold?' She looked away. Her skin was prickling, her heart was beating so hard she felt in danger of passing out, her mouth was dry and her head was throbbing.

'Practical.'

'No, it's not *practical*, Luca! Packing sunblock when you go on holiday to a hot country is *practical*! Being ice-cold and having no emotions…' She gazed at him helplessly.

'I saw what my mother's death did to my father,' Luca grated. 'I think I've told you this already.'

'Doesn't mean I agree with you!'

'He never recovered. You'd have to be a fool to let yourself feel so strongly for another human being that you end up losing your way if something happens to them! And after she died? Let's not forget that I witnessed first-hand how callous and greedy women could be when it came to money. Hell, I was just a teenager at the time, but there were some who didn't think twice about trying it on with me when their advances hit a dead end with my father!'

'You'd rather spend the rest of your life being lonely than take a chance?' Ellie was pleading. She could hear it in her voice and it shamed her.

'I've never been lonely in my life.'

'I'm not talking about having a woman in your bed! I'm talking about having a woman in your heart!'

'I'll take my chances on being just fine without that complication.'

'Right.' She leapt to her feet. Tears were stinging the back of her eyes but there was no way that she was going to let him see her break down in front of him. 'I think it's a good time for me to head upstairs.'

'Ellie…'

'Don't say anything else, Luca.' She spun round on her heels and headed straight for the kitchen door. No way was she going to get up early tomorrow to bid a fond farewell to her sister. She'd be seeing her soon enough, and how Lily was going to have a bit of fun at her expense.

Strangely, Ellie didn't care.

She couldn't hurt worse than she was hurting right now.

She had become accustomed to sleeping with Luca. She almost went to his bedroom through force of habit. Instead, she swerved and quietly let herself into her own bedroom.

Her suitcase was stuffed in the wardrobe and she pulled it out and opened it. When she had packed to come over, she had been filled with excitement and trepidation. It had felt like the greatest adventure of her life.

Now, she looked at that suitcase and knew that this

time, when she was packing it, she would be filled with misery.

She had no idea how long she'd been stuffing clothes into the case, but the knock on the door carried the impact of a hand grenade because she knew who it was going to be. Lily might have scuttled out of the kitchen when faced with Luca, but her curiosity would be boundless, and Ellie knew that she probably would have heard her coming up the stairs.

She hurriedly flung the suitcase into the wardrobe and composed herself into the image of a woman in love who, mysteriously, was not sharing a bedroom with the guy she was supposedly all set to marry.

She was smiling as she pulled open the door. It was a rictus smile but it was the best she could muster given the circumstances.

She expected Lily with a list of questions.

She got Luca.

She didn't budge.

'Let me in, Ellie.'

'Go away.'

'What are you doing?' He peered around her and Ellie followed his gaze to the half-open wardrobe.

'Packing.'

'Let me in.' Luca shifted uneasily, raked his fingers through his hair. 'Please. I… I've been a fool, Ellie.'

'Really?' Her voice was the temperature of ice. 'I thought that was my terrain.'

'I was a fool,' Luca muttered with low urgency, 'to think that I could live without you.'

Their eyes tangled and Ellie glared at him.

'Right. And I'm supposed to believe that?'

'I don't want to have this conversation with you out

here.' He shuffled when she didn't say anything. 'I've never begged for anything in my life. I'm not sure I'd know how but, if you don't let me in, then I'm going to have to give it a go.'

Ellie stood aside with visible reluctance and, as soon as he was in the bedroom and the door was shut, she removed herself to the broad window sill and perched against it with her arms folded, staring at him.

Undeterred, Luca positioned himself right next to her. 'You told me you loved me.'

'I don't want to be reminded of that,' Ellie muttered viciously.

'You told me that you loved me and I did what came naturally to me. I turned away. It's the way I've been programmed. My life was as placid as a lake until you swept in like a whirlwind, breathing brimstone and fire. You didn't care what I thought. You said whatever you wanted to say and I had no idea how addictive that would become.'

'If you're saying all that to butter me up into re-considering the engagement thing for Jake's sake, then forget it.'

'If I were terrified of being with a woman who loved me, then there's no way I would be considering any engagement, Jake or no Jake.'

'Just say what you have to say, Luca.' Hope was beginning to send out alarming tendrils and, before they became too profuse, Ellie wanted him to spit it out.

'I thought that there was strength in building an ivory tower around myself,' he said quietly. 'I was protected and no one had ever been able to breach my ramparts. And then along you came and you managed to find a way through within seconds. I asked you to come out here because I needed you to be here for Jake—but where I would have been cautious about having any woman around, sharing my space for that length of time and in that capacity, with you I felt…comfortable.'

'Comfortable.' Why did that word sound so…*dull and boring*?

Luca laughed. 'It's a compliment, Ellie. It's also something that should have alerted me to the fact that you weren't just different from the women I've known. It should have alerted me to the fact that I was falling for you.'

'Falling for me…? Is that why you listened to me pour my heart out and then sent me on my way?'

'Like I said, I responded on cue. A lifetime of telling myself that love was the one thing I didn't do swung into action. I'd say I was shocked by what you said, but in fact I wasn't. I'd say I felt trapped, but no, that would be a lie as well. As soon as you walked out of the kitchen, I felt sick.'

'But you never let on…'

'I didn't have it in me and, anyway, I didn't recognise the signposts because I'd never walked down that road before and I'd never wanted to. Honestly, I didn't get the appeal,' he confessed with wrenching honesty. 'You were nothing like what I was used to and, to start with, I just figured that you were different, that you were a tonic for my jaded palate, but then we slept together and you blew me away.'

'You blew me away, too.' Ellie rested her hand on his chest and felt the fast beating of his heart. 'I guess I was as rigid in what I wanted as you were. I guess some of that was down to my own insecurities. If I didn't punch above my weight then I would never be let down. Lily is the one who gets the good-looking guys, and I told my-self that that was fine because I wasn't attracted to that sort anyway. When I met you, you were the last person I thought I could ever have a connection with.'

'I'll bet.' Luca smiled crookedly. He covered her hand with his, lifted it to his lips and dropped a kiss on her palm. 'We didn't exactly meet in circumstances that cast a glowing halo around me, did we? I can only imag-ine what you were thinking. Arrogant bastard, too much money, runaway kid...'

'But I still couldn't take my eyes off you, Luca. You mesmerised me and I hated it. It's like I wasn't really alive until you came along and then, boom, life was Tech-nicolor-bright.' She sighed. 'You made me face all the old insecurities and come to terms with them, and finally you made me overcome them.'

'And you, my darling, made me realise that life isn't worth living unless you're prepared to take chances.' He swept her off her feet, carried her to the bed and gently deposited her as though she was as fragile as porcelain. Then he stood back and looked at her for long minutes before sliding into bed next to her and immediately curv-ing her towards him so that their bodies were pressed against one another.

'So...can I ask you that question once again?'

'What question?' As if she didn't know. Ellie squirmed against him, fingers itching to rip his clothes off.

'Will you marry me? For real? Because I can't con-template a life without you. I want you to be there for me, for Jake and for all the kids we're going to have together. I love you, *querida*, now and for ever...'

'How,' Ellie laughed, 'is a girl supposed to say no to a proposal like that?'

* * *

It was a fairy-tale story for avid reporters and, for the first time in his life, Luca actually gave them what they wanted because he was just so proud to show off the woman who was going to be his wife.

They were married without fanfare in the local church in the village where Ellie had grown up although several days later, and before they departed on their honeymoon to the Maldives, they threw a bash worthy of any A-lister to celebrate their union.

And not only were her father and all her friends in attendance, but so was her sister.

She and Lily had had a long talk when they had finally met up back in the UK and Ellie had been startled to learn that for every insecurity she had had, her sister likewise had her own.

'You were so bright,' Lily had admitted. 'I could never get higher than a C but you were a straight-A student and sometimes it felt as though Dad only had eyes for you. I could slog my guts out and I knew I'd still never be able to make it to university. It was easier in the end to just let Mum have her way and, you know... I got accustomed to making the most of my looks. But your brains will last for ever. My looks won't and I know that.'

Then it had all come out in an outpouring of emotion that had left Ellie feeling closer to her sister than she had in a very long time.

Lily had gone to seek fame and fortune but instead she had just joined the quagmire of hopefuls all out there looking for the same thing. She'd become just one of many pretty faces trying to clamber up the same tree.

'I ran out of money,' she'd admitted. 'That's why I couldn't send any over for Dad. I had none. I was waitressing by night and then going round and round, looking for agents, trying to get hold of connections. Everyone was doing the same thing. You wouldn't believe what it's like…'

The steps Jake had made in forming a bond with Luca had been quite remarkable. The memories of his parents would never leave him; Ellie knew that. But he was no longer the lost child who had felt the need to run as fast and as far as he could from a place he didn't like.

And the Maldives…

Ellie looked at the wedding band on her finger and smiled. Sitting out here, with an orange sunset dropping over sea that was as calm as a lake, she almost had to pinch herself that she wasn't playing the lead role in a dream, one from which she would cruelly awaken at any minute.

Back in England, Jake was with her father and her sister, who had given up dreams of stardom and was slowly realising that there was a lot to be said for ordinary.

Here… She swivelled around and absorbed the stunning scenery. Rich foliage was bathed in a mellow light cast by strings of lanterns that zip-lined through the trees and shivered and twinkled in the lazy evening breeze. The sound of invisible insects was a background orchestra of soothing sounds. Ahead, the dark sea was as flat as glass. It was hard to believe that, as soon as dawn broke, that black body of smooth water would become turquoise and alive with colourful fish.

The place was paradise but what made it really special was the fact that she was here with her husband.

She heard Luca behind her and turned around, smiling and already tingling because he never failed to impress her. He was just so spectacular, prowling with the grace and strength of a panther. And hers! She felt a hot flare of possessiveness.

Their two-bedroom cabin was the height of luxury and so secluded that they could practically walk around naked without fear of being seen. But right now, fresh from a shower, he had a towel slung low on his lean hips.

His hair was still damp and he raked his fingers through it then stood behind her before inclining to slip his hands underneath the silk strappy dress, finding her bare breasts and gently massaging them.

Ellie squirmed and twisted round then knelt on the chair so that she could hold his face in her hands and kiss him.

'Sometimes I can't believe it's possible to be so happy,' she murmured and Luca smiled.

'Nor can I,' he admitted. He sauntered round to sit next to her on the padded two-seater on the wooden deck of their cabin.

'You were the man who felt claustrophobic at the thought of a woman cooking for you,' she teased, holding his hand and linking her fingers through his. 'Remember?'

'How could I forget when you got me an apron saying "domesticated and proud of it" to show me the error of my ways?'

'You never wear that apron.' She sighed, smiling.

'I wouldn't want to invade your territory. I know you like cooking for me so why spoil your fun?'

Ellie burst out laughing. He didn't wear the apron but he could cook a mean steak.

'I look back at the man I used to be, afraid of letting go in case I got hurt, and I marvel that I could ever have been so short-sighted. Although, maybe I was just waiting for the right woman to come along and show me the error of my ways...' He pulled her towards him and kissed the tip of her nose, then covered her mouth with his, stroking her rib cage and firing her up so that she just wanted to haul him back into the cabin so that she could have her wicked way with him.

'And now that we're married,' he continued with a smile in his voice, 'maybe it's time we took this to the next level...'

'Next level?'

'I think it's time for Jake to have a sibling, don't you?' He chuckled and then swung round the chair so that he could hoist her into his arms, caveman style, carry her back into the cabin and into the bedroom with its four-poster bed. 'And why put off for tomorrow what can be done today?' His grin was wicked as she began stripping off the slip of a dress under which she was completely naked.

'Just today?' she teased.

'Today,' Luca said with tenderness, 'tomorrow and every day for the rest our lives.'

\* \* \* \* \*

# LET'S TALK

# Romance

For exclusive extracts, competitions
and special offers, find us online:

- **f** facebook.com/millsandboon
- **⊙** @millsandboonuk
- **🐦** @millsandboon

Or get in touch on 0844 844 1351*

For all the latest titles coming soon,
visit millsandboon.co.uk/nextmonth